Everything's Coming Up Roses
Copyright©2014 Barry Lowe
ISBN 978-1-909934-82-5
Cover art and design by Dawné Dominique

Published by
Lydian Press 2014
Find us on the World Wide Web at
www.lydianpress.com

EVERYTHING'S COMING UP ROSES

Four Tales of M/M Romance

Barry Lowe

Lydian Press

CONTENTS

All previously published as individual eBooks by Lydian Press

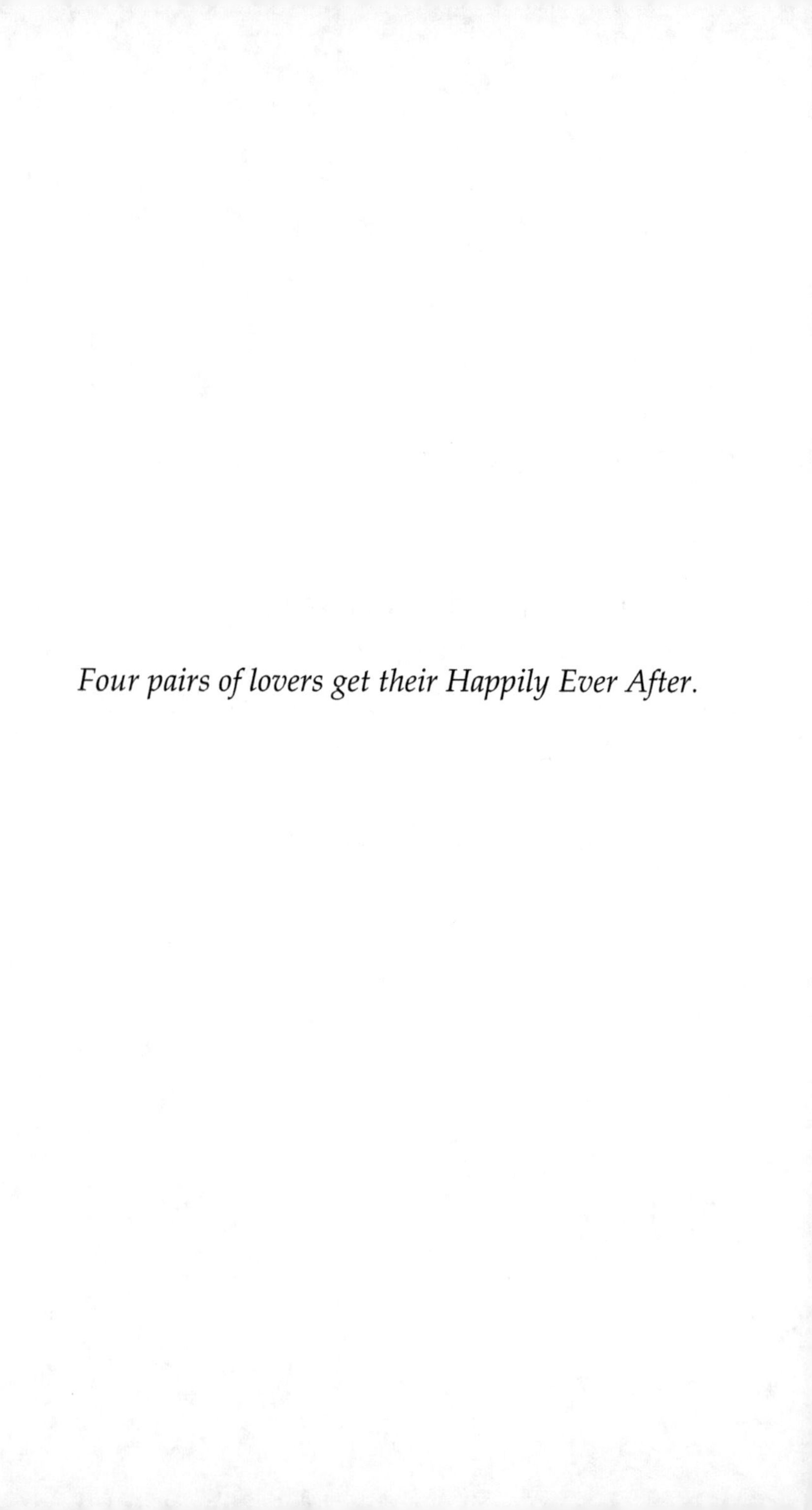

Four pairs of lovers get their Happily Ever After.

THE DAY OF THE CLIFFORDS

When a day that you happen to know is Saturday starts off by sounding like the end of the world, there is something seriously wrong somewhere. The noise woke me from a troubled sleep. I was exhausted from weeks of stress. The previous day I'd buried my nan, the woman who had brought me up after the accident that claimed my parents when I was a little nipper of ten. I have scant memory of my parents; the woman holding me in her arms in the only photographs I have of them is a stranger, the man giving me a piggy back in another even more so because the occasions on which he had time to play with me were fewer. They were the two people who brought me into the world, but it was my nan who brought me up.

I watched her deteriorate as the cancer took hold of her body and won the battle. She'd fought valiantly but age and fatigue were not the best allies to have. The day before she succumbed, she took my hand, squeezed it, and whispered, "It's much too hard to go on. I've had a good life. It's time for you to have yours, Samuel Peter Dempsey. Make it count."

Nan dropped off to sleep after that and never spoke again.

So the raucous music and the shouts and swearing emanating from the house next door seemed somehow to be a slight on her memory. She would not have put up with it; she would have been at the wooden fence separating the two properties shouting for them to quieten down. At seventy-six, she was not to be taken lightly and you under-estimated her at your peril. But, I was not my grandmother.

Fumbling beside the bed, I found the switch for the lamp on the bedside table. The old clock showed it was two o'clock. It was outrageous that people could make so much racket this time of the morning. I didn't want to make a fuss about it but the whump whump whump of the bass line of the music vibrated off the walls, doing my head in. I longed for the old days when the Fittons lived next door; a couple a generation younger than my nan who would look in on her each day to ensure she was all right before I moved back about two years ago to care for her full-time. It was a reversal of roles for she'd cared for me as a boy and young man.

I remembered the day she'd come to the city to claim me with my sullen expression and my equally sullen suitcase of clothes and toys, including my beloved teddy bear Clive who, if truth be known, was even more sullen than me to be uprooted from his comfortable existence in the outer suburbs of the city to be transplanted to Lakesmouth, the considerably smaller holiday township squeezed onto an isthmus of sand and scrub between the ocean to the east and the large Lake Columbine to the west.

It was the 1950s and my new school was to be a tiny one-teacher weatherboard building on a giant allotment of pampas grass; the disparate students all mixed in together like raisins, sultanas and glacé fruit in a plum pudding. My education felt similar, a hodge-podge of history, geography, maths, and English. After the luxury of a separate class for each year in my former primary school, Lakesmouth North Primary came as a shock. Added to that, the locals didn't take kindly to a newcomer from the city and let it be known. The first six months was an experience I would never like to repeat.

My nan, smelling of the dark chocolate she kept hidden in the drawers of her old Victorian wardrobe, would clutch me to her ample bosom, kiss me on the top of the head and, miraculously, everything would be better. It wasn't until I was old enough to attend high school that things did improve. By that stage I was savvy enough to know I had little interest in the pursuits that most of my fellow classmates had decided upon. They dreamed small: taking over the family fish and chips shop down by the beach, or driving one of the local buses that shuddered from the nearest railway station twelve miles away to the holiday town that swelled to almost double with fun-seeking tourists every summer brought up from the Big Smoke on the coal-powered locomotives that filled the air with soot and hot steel.

And every summer the carnival came to town, setting up just south of the bridge on a flat area filled with picnic tables and changing facilities for those daring enough to wade out into the fast flowing channel carrying the lake into the sea. I would nag my nan to take me on the Ghost Train, or through the Mirror Maze, or up high on the Ferris wheel so I could look down on all the tiny ant people below. At that young age everything was so much bigger, so by the time I turned fifteen I was over most aspects of the sideshow except for the men with their sleeves rolled up to show their muscles, or the men who wore tank tops that revealed their tanned necks and arms with a peep of arm-pit hair, or else the boxers in gold dressings gowns who would stand aloof as a carney spruiked their lethal fighting ability, challenging any local stupid enough to take on the champ for a pocket of small change if he miraculously won. I would stand mesmerized until the boxer removed his dressing gown, hoping he'd have a body of rippling muscles to the awe of the crowd and the erection enticing excitement of yours truly.

Of course, the majority of these men didn't have top bodies. They were older men gone to pot, with cauliflower ears, bellies that cascaded over their gaudy shorts, their ability as false as their names; Tornado Tommy or Cyclone Colin or, just plain, The Killer. I never went inside to watch the reality of fights, preferring the fantasy in my mind of two sweaty men grappling in semi-naked combat.

By the time I reached fifteen, nan had decided I was safe enough on my own and merely ladled out a small amount of her hard-earned cash so that I could have a little fun if I was careful, or else I could stand with a few of the locals in the pinball parlor. Watching older teens attempting to pick up girls was free although the accompanying pop music soundtrack of Del Shannon, Helen Shapiro, Roy Orbison, Neil Sedaka, and Bobby Vee, required a shilling in the slot of the Wurlitzer jukebox.

Well before my curfew time of midnight, I would trudge back across the old wooden bridge to home where nan would be lying in her heavy Victorian double bed that I'd needed a chair to help me clamber into as a boy because it was so high off the floor, a crossword puzzle in her hands, the well-thumbed dictionary open beside her, or else her Bible over which she'd be praying for the souls of my parents or for protection for me as I grew into adulthood. I knew it was already too late – I was damned because I didn't seem to find girls to my liking. Not like the other boys in my class who did everything to lure them behind the toilet block after school to kiss them. I always wondered what it would be like to kiss a boy. I never wondered what it would be like to kiss a girl.

I almost found out one sweltering night as I walked from the pinball parlor along the town's main street to the bridge. A young guy, blond hair, multi-colored singlet and Hawaiian shorts, wearing flip flops, fell in step alongside me. I'd seen him in the pinball parlor, his arm around one of the local high school girls who, I'd heard the rumors, put out for hot surfers from the city. This guy was hot. He was tanned to a luscious toast color; his arms were sinewy with nuggety biceps and powerful shoulders. His legs were covered by a series of saltwater bleached hairs that stood out against his brown skin. I wanted so much to be the girl he had his arm around.

I had no idea what it all meant. My emotional experience was zilch, my sexual experience little more than jerking off as quietly as possible because my nan was in the next room and the walls were fibro thin. She'd had the talk about self-pollution and sin although her condemnation of the practice was insufficient to get me to stop. Something as esoteric as sin versus the instant gratification of masturbation? It was a no-brainer: orgasm won hands down every time. That was the sum total of my sexual education. This was the era of Frankie and Annette and Beach Party Virginity.

I relaxed when he told me his name was Rory, that he was staying in the caravan park with his mates and he was walking home because he needed to be up early the next morning to 'catch some waves.' I smelled beer. My nan frowned on alcohol although she was known to take the occasional medicinal sip of brandy, which she hated purchasing from the town's one and only bottle shop. She would never enter a pub. The medicinal brandy, tempered with warm water and sugar, was always doled out to me when I had a cold, and I developed a liking for it as a cure, so much so that I still dose myself up with it at the first sign of sniffles.

Beer, she considered vulgar. On Rory, however, it smelled like the best cologne in the world. He wasn't exactly handsome, his face was too angular for that, but he wasn't ugly. He sported stubble on his chin and a sort of wispy moustache that threatened to blow away in a good breeze it looked so sparse. He caught me looking at him.

"You're a good-looking fucker," he said, thrilling me with his use of profanity. My grandmother had a lexicon of words which were forbidden, including the usual culprits although she also considered a word such as 'passion' not one that could be used in polite company. I'd made the mistake of telling her I'd put a coin in a slot machine in the pinball arcade that supposedly told your character type by merely holding on to a metal handle. Mine just happened to come up 'passionate.' When I informed nan proudly, she was horrified. She equated passion with excessive sex. Considering she'd married a man twenty years her senior and had produced just one child, my mum, I assumed passion was in short supply in her life.

Passion, thereafter, became my guilty secret. Rory, for example.

He was all jokes and mateship, drawing me in as if we were long lost buddies. Much too casually to have been anything but rehearsed, he said, just as we approached the bridge, "Do ever play with yourself?" He made it seem like a conspiracy between two men. I genuinely liked the guy. He was the sort of older friend I'd always wanted; especially if he was my 'in' to the group of more popular surf dudes who hung around the streets and pinball parlors at night. Yeah, I was naïve.

My throat suddenly got dry and it was difficult to swallow. Thinking it must be some sort of test, I decided to brave the truth. "Yeah," I croaked.

"It's good, isn't it?"

I put a little more enthusiasm into my next monosyllabic reply. "Yeah."

"You ever do it with your mates?"

My answer stretched the truth only a little. "Yeah."

I was already so stiff in my shorts it was quite obvious. As was the tent in Rory's board shorts.

"You wanna help me out?"

My response was a little more enthusiastic this time. "Sure."

We were almost at the end of the old bridge. "Come on," he whispered, leading me off and under the wooden planks that rattled whenever a car drove across. There was a boat shed at the water's edge that hired to local tourists and fishermen, and did a lucrative sideline in selling bait and renting out fishing gear, that provided cover for our activities.

Rory didn't exactly kiss me – at least not on the mouth. In fact, he remained fully clothed while he dropped to his knees, yanked down my shorts, and quickly engulfed my hard prick in his mouth. "What are you doing?" I whimpered.

He was forced to take his mouth off my cock to reply and appeared none-too-pleased. "What's it look like I'm doing? I'm sucking your cock." He wrapped his lips around my throbbing cock and I hissed, "Sweet Jesus."

He stopped again. "Have you never had your cock sucked before?"

I shook my head, scared he might think better of continuing. However, he seemed pleased by the information, paying my dick even more attention than before. I wasn't going to last long and within minutes I was tapping him on the shoulder, trying to squeeze my excitement back into my body. "Um, Rory," I groaned. "I think I'm…" Too late! My spunk blew into Rory's mouth and he swallowed, licking every last drop from my prick. He leaned back on his heels, wiped his mouth, and smiled up at me. "Virgin spunk. Sweet as."

Panic gripped me. I hoped he didn't want me to reciprocate because I thought what he'd just done was disgusting. It was all very well two mates wanking each other's pricks but putting it in your mouth? Erk. I tugged up my shorts as fast as I could and made a dash for it, not stopping for breath until I reached the safety of nan's house. Allowing myself a quick glance back along the street to ascertain I hadn't been followed, I retrieved the key from under the back-door mat, letting myself in quietly, hoping to catch my breath before the inevitable inquisition on what I'd been doing that evening. I didn't think telling nan I'd just had my cock sucked by another man was a good idea.

I went to the kitchen to get a glass of water, calling, "You want a cup of tea, nan?" I knew she never drank just before going to sleep because she'd be up all night but it gave me an opportunity to straighten my clothes and calm myself down. My emotions were like scattershot through my mind and body. I was both appalled and excited by what had just happened; I would have trouble looking nan in the eye, but somehow I managed. I kissed her on the cheek, telling her I was tired, which was not a total lie, I just didn't mention it was because I'd run most of the way home.

I guess I was still flushed in the face because she looked at me forensically. Feeling I had to say something, I muttered about how warm it was outside. I escaped to my bedroom, ensuring the door was closed tight so I could strip off and examine my penis. It was still intact, no teeth marks on the skin. I breathed easy, but just so

I didn't run into Rory again, I stayed home for the next week, using the excuse that night life in Lakesmouth was rather monotonous at this time of year. Nan was probably relived that she didn't have to hand over any more cash for my pinball parlor addiction.

As the days and weeks passed and I went back to my old night habits, my brief encounter with Rory took on an added romantic sheen that was totally fictitious. I began to crave a repeat of the experience but, of course, Rory was long gone. I would have to find someone else.

THE EXCESSIVE noise from the party next door was beginning to give me a headache. I'm as big a party animal as anyone else but enough is enough. I was surprised no one had called the cops as yet although knowing the local constabulary they would just pass the buck onto the local council rangers. I suspected, though, the locals had merely shut their windows and closed their curtains to damp down the sounds which were a common enough intrusion in the holiday season. I would have done the same had it not been for nan's funeral. I wanted to grieve and that's almost impossible with the thump of dance music. You need peace and quiet, a sense of calm, to grieve. What I had was David Bowie, T-Rex, The Bay City Rollers, and Blondie.

Sighing, I got out of bed, wrapping myself in the first loose-fitting clothing I came across and went outside to see if I could get them to lower the volume to a respectable level. I trudged around to their front door which, fortuitously for me, was open, as I doubt they would have heard me knock. I did try rapping my knuckles against the fibro wall next to the door but it was to no avail. I repeated the exercise adding a shout of 'hello' to the mix. After a few futile attempts to attract somebody's attention, I gave up and pulled open the fly-screen door to enter the premises. Once inside, I stood watching a group of about a dozen people around my age hedonistically smoking, drinking, and chatting at the top of their voice in order to be heard over the raucous background soundtrack.

No one noticed me even after coughing loudly and again calling my greeting. There was only one solution. I went to the stereo to turn down the sound. Conversation stopped immediately and all eyes turned in my direction.

"What the…?" a male exclaimed from another room, the partygoers making way for his entrance. He glared at me for a moment. "Who the fuck are you?"

I was too startled to answer but I saw the look of recognition slowly filter across his face. "Oh my God." We both said it at the same time.

The man staring at me open-mouthed was the last person I ever expected to see again. It was Jerry Clifford

– as large as life and twice as gorgeous as I'd ever seen him before.

"What's it been?" he asked.

"Ten years, give or take a week."

One of the young women went to stand beside Jerry in an obvious act of proprietorship. Jerry put his arm around her shoulder as if to shield himself from any thoughts I might have about him. I had plenty. Jerry Clifford had been my first crush.

I was fourteen when I first met him. He and his younger brother, Matt, came up from the city to spend summer school holidays with the Fittons, their grandparents. That first year we were wary of each other. The ice had been broken by Matt wandering into our backyard in search of Pearl, the Fittons' Staffordshire, who had a tendency to chase after nan's chooks. The hens were given free access to the backyard during daylight hours to root through our small garden to pick off any bugs and snails that dared trespass on her veggies. At night they found safety inside their specially constructed shed enclosed by wire mesh. Every now and then Pearl would find a loose paling in the fence and squeeze her way through, wreaking havoc on the usual equanimity of the poor egg layers. Nan would usually scare Pearl away with the help of a large straw broom and a scream of, "Come and get your bloody dog," directed at the Fittons' house.

I suspect the Fittons sat inside watching her in full flight, huffing and puffing in pursuit of a crazy dog. Eventually, nan would run out of breath and retire exhausted to the back step. Mr. Fitton would then open his back door and shout "What's all the commotion?" before whistling to Pearl who then bounded back into the correct yard as if nothing untoward had happened. The world would then slip back onto its proper axis when nan shouted, "Your bloody dog will be the death of me."

It was one of those rare days when nan had gone to visit friends; a group of women her own age who liked to play bingo every Wednesday afternoon. I heard the hens' terrified squawking and I knew chookageddon was in progress. The sound reminded me a little too much of the occasions upon which my grandmother, sleeves rolled up, hatchet in hand as she rounded up one of the hens, dispatched it with one swift decapitation. I'd made the mistake of watching once. Thereafter, I raced inside the house, blocking my ears with my fingers, scrunching my eyes closed tightly as I sat backed into the farthest corner of my nan's dark wardrobe in an attempt to escape the squawks of death.

As I was alone it was up to me to deflect Pearl before she could do any damage. I ran out the back door, slamming the screen behind me because the flies were terrible that year and nan didn't like to use the pressure pack sprays because it gave her an attack of the sneezes because she inevitably used half a can on the poor buggers that managed to find their way into the house.

Talk about overkill.

Pearl barked in delight at the mayhem she was causing, while a young boy called after her over the side fence in a futile effort to get her to heel. No way could I use the straw broom to scare off Pearl: it was too big for me to wield threateningly. However, I'd long ago perfected Mr. Fittons' whistle. Pearl came bounding over to lick my face and I'd managed to calm her down before leashing her to walk her next door just as the young kid, about eleven or twelve years old, raced around the corner calling the dog. He stopped short when he saw me. "Who are you?" he asked shyly.

"I'm Sam. I live here with my nan. Who are you?"

"Matthew Clifford," he answered grandly, puffing his body up to its full height which was still considerably shorter than me seated on the step. "My friends call me Matt or Matty."

"Then I shall call you Matt as well."

He seemed unsure. "O-kay."

I patted the step beside me. He approached cautiously but sat himself down and began to pat the dog who obviously thought she was in doggy heaven with all the attention, thumping her tail against the cement path.

"I've seen another boy around the house. Is he your brother?" I enquired.

Matt wrinkled his nose as if he smelled something bad. "That's Jeremy. He's my older brother. I don't like him because he treats me like a child. Thinks he's too grown up to play with me. You won't treat me like a child, will you, Sam?"

His young eyes pleaded with me so it would have been remiss of me not to give in. I grabbed him around the neck to noogie his hair. "I'll treat you like the grown-up you are."

Matt squealed with delight and wriggled out of my grip just as a boy around my age, fourteen, came into the yard. "There you are," he said, glaring at Matty. "I can't leave you alone for a minute."

"Hi," I said, my voice catching at the sight of the blond Adonis. Here was the boy of my dreams, not that I knew what my dreams signified at that stage. All I knew was that I would walk across broken glass in my bare feet if he asked. I wanted to be his friend. I ignored the tingle in my groin because I had just reached puberty but had no concept of sexual attraction as yet. Matt looked at my face and then at Jeremy. "He's my friend. I saw him first."

"He's too old for you," Jeremy said with a superior air. "You take Pearl back inside."

"What are you going to do?" Matt asked.

"None of your business," Jeremy snarled. "I'll be in later. Now scoot."

Matt was dejected. "Come on, Pearl." The dog followed him. Before he disappeared around the side of the house, Matt turned on his older brother, "You always spoil everything."

I couldn't let him go away like that. I called, "I'll see you later, Matt." That cheered him up and he ran off with Pearl chasing after him.

"You'll be sorry you said that," Jeremy said.

"Jeremy, eh?"

"Unless you want your teeth rearranged, it's Jerry."

"Got it," I said.

We sat and made small talk until my nan came home. She invited us both in for ice cream over which she gave him the third degree. He and Matt had no other siblings and from now on would be taken in by the Fittons every summer school holidays to give their parents a rest. Years later, I discovered Matt's parents were trying to add a little sister to the family and the couple of weeks a year when they offloaded their two sons gave them their only opportunity for privacy in order to try.

Jerry was smart enough to be on his best behavior, playing up to my nan who was suspicious of anyone new. By the end of the ice cream treat she was a fan. Even more so of Matty when he knocked on the door and whined through the fly screen, "Gran said it's time for you to come home, Jeremy. Tea is almost ready."

"Who have we here?" nan said, opening the door to usher him it. Matt went quiet, his shyness muting his tongue.

"That's Matty," I said. "He's my new friend from next door."

Matt looked pleased with my description but Jerry had to puncture it. "He's my really annoying little brother."

That started them bickering, threatening to become an all-out war until nan stepped in to calm them both down. Not long after, they left to have their dinner. "Looks as if you've made some new friends," nan said. "Though I think you may have to see them separately. I've never seen two brothers at such loggerheads before."

I felt pretty superior at that stage because I sensed their animosity had to do with me and which of them was going to be Friend Number One. I spent time with Matt who developed a strong case of hero worship, probably as a result of my treating him as an equal rather than talking down to him like I heard Jerry and his grandparents. I guess I felt sorry for him because there were no kids his own age to play with, and I sort of identified with what it was like to be Matt's age and have no one to talk to. It was the story of my life when I first arrived at Lakesmouth.

Still, I favored Jerry in every other respect and I idolized him. Attraction hit me with the same force as running into a brick wall, and I discovered many years later my condition had a name: homosexuality. It wasn't talked about in polite society. I only ever heard it spoken of in whispers and then usually associated with the word 'sin.' I tried bringing the subject up with nan when I was sixteen, telling her I'd overheard older boys in the playground at high school mention the word. Her response was succinct, brooking no argument. "They're just disgusting old men who can't get a woman." For a split second I thought she was being satirical, but no, she was deadly serious. "It's nothing to worry yourself about, Sammy. You're a sensible boy. If some strange man offers you lollies and asks you to get into his car, just scream. That'll send him packing."

Even at my young age, I knew her opinion was so old fashioned it was borderline dangerous. The one thing I did learn from our talk, however, was to keep my mouth shut. Nan went to her grave not knowing that her grandson had been experimenting with the young man from next door during the school holidays and had learned everything he knew from the 'nice young farmer' (as she called him) who ran the fruit and vegetable co-op in Lakesmouth's main street where she did her shopping.

It was Jerry first taught me about masturbation: he called it wanking, my nan called it self-pollution. Jerry and I had gone to the surf beach together, leaving Matt behind, in order to talk about 'boy things.' We became close friends, sharing our best-kept secrets, so it was inevitable that anything we discovered in the realm of sexuality was shared. The one thing I kept to myself was that I fancied him.

"You got hair around your willy?" Jerry asked as we lay on our towels soaking up the sun. We'd discovered our own little semi-private corner of the sand hills that overlooked the vast expanse that made up Lakesmouth North Beach. Not many people used it apart from a few intrepid board riders because it had no life savers or surf club. People who ventured into the water did so at their own peril, the surf notorious for rips and changing currents.

From our vantage point we could see anyone approaching before they'd spot us in the sand. The privacy was conducive to sex talk.

"Yeah," I replied. "Started about a year ago."

"You get hard all the time?"

"Uh huh. What about you?"

"I'm hard now," he said.

My eyes immediately went to the small tent in the front of his Speedos. My excitement was just as obvious.

In a voice squeaky with longing, I said, "Show me."

"Okay, but you gotta show me yours as well."

I tried to sound reluctant. "Okay."

"On the count of three. One. Two. Three."

I whipped my swimmers off but he'd baulked when his were down over his butt but snagged on his erection.

"Not fair," I said, gamely leaning over to wrest them all the way down so he was as naked as I was.

We both tried not to look at each other but I knew we were both comparing sizes. We were about equal in that department even though I was a skinny runt and he was much beefier and more muscular as a result of playing high school sport.

"You ever kissed a girl?" he asked.

"Nah," I replied. When his silence intimated I'd better have a real good excuse, I added, "The girls around here are real dogs. I'm waiting until the tourists flood in. I'm gonna get me a girlfriend who puts out."

"Wow. Cool."

"Have you kissed a girl?"

"Only my cousin, Heather."

"How was it?"

"Cool."

I wondered if he really had kissed his cousin because his response seemed remarkably skimpy on detail.

There was a catch in his voice. "It got me really hard." He began stroking his dick, his hand moving up and down the shaft. "You ever wanked till you come?"

My sex education was sadly lacking at this stage. Of course, I'd heard about masturbation, but not the mechanics. It was associated with sin, and sin I was assured, would consign me to hell. "No," I admitted. "How do you do that?"

"You just pull your cock like I'm doing until this milky spunk shoots out the end. Look, I'll show you."

I couldn't believe my luck; I had the perfect excuse to stare at Jerry's cock without having to hide my obvious interest, although I would have liked nothing better than to reach over and help him out. I had enough sense to realize that was a reach too far.

As he turned red in the face and his breath came in pants, I played with my own dick which was harder than I ever remembered it being before. A few minutes later, Jerry was wriggling and moaning like he was having some sort of fit and I prepared to run off to get help, but then he gasped, "Here it comes" and a wad of cream spurted out the end of his dick splatting on his chest, followed by another and another until he shuddered and he sank back onto his towel as if he were exhausted.

I was gob smacked. "What does it feel like?"

"The best feeling you'll ever have." He had a crazy, self-satisfied smirk on his face. "You should try it. The first time takes forever but when it happens. Oh, boy."

Jerry raced down to the water's edge and tumbled in the surf to clean off the puddles of spunk. I pulled my Speedos up and when he returned we lay back to discuss seemingly earth-shattering topics such as the latest movies and television shows we watched. We were both into vampires and monsters and space aliens. At our age the future seemed a long way off.

Later, as we walked back to our respective homes, Jerry offered me some manly advice. "If your nan has some cold cream or there's a jar of Vaseline in the laundry, put some in the palm of your hand, it makes it feel better. The secret is to keep going. Your arm might ache but it's worth it in the long run, no matter how long it takes. And, um, make sure you have some Kleenex handy to wipe it up. If you do it in a hankie or an old sock, it smells. Your nan will know what you're up to. Best to flush it down the toilet."

It was good to have a friend like Jerry looking out for my interests. In the end, I used suntan lotion because my nan didn't leave any cold cream lying about and there was no Vaseline in the laundry or the back garden shed. It seemed to do the trick. I had the tissues ready as I set out on my new adventure. Had this been a road trip, I think I would have given up and gone back home long before I reached my destination but, because it had to do with my dick, I kept going, changing hands when one arm threatened to cramp from the repetitive action. I was in a hurry that first time not knowing what to expect.

It began as a throb, then a tingle, and then this great upheaval in my hormones, my balls gripping in preparation for my first ejaculation. When it spewed out, the feeling was so intense I thought I'd die. I wasn't exactly a man but I sure felt like one. I wiped my stomach and my hand of the sticky mess, wondering briefly what it tasted like but, thinking it might be toxic, I flushed it down the toilet. By the time I got back to bed, I wanted to try it again.

Jerry and I spent the remainder of the holidays avoiding his little brother who simply refused to be sidelined, and jerking off in front of each other. There was no touching involved even though I was adamant that before Jerry went back to the city I was going to get my hands on his prick. I probably would have too if Matty hadn't discovered our hideaway in the sand hills.

Fortunately, we'd both blown our second or third load of the morning and had wiped ourselves clean, settling back on our towels to sun bake and shoot the breeze when a shadow fell over us.

"So this is where you get to," a pissed-off voice said. Matty looked at me accusingly. "I thought you were my friend too."

"I am, Matt," I explained. "It's just Jerry and I sometimes want to be alone to talk man talk."

"I can talk man talk," he pouted.

"No, you can't," Jerry snapped. "When you get older you'll understand."

Matty looked triumphant. "I understand more than you think. I know you steal nana's face cream, and I'll tell her if you don't let me play."

Jerry sighed. I tried hard to suppress an attack of the giggles because Matty looked so serious standing there, hands on his hips, defying his older brother. He must have seen the grin on my face before I had time to disguise it because he smirked at me, and winked. The little bugger was blackmailing us.

Jerry picked up his towel and stormed off down the beach, muttering, "You're just a fuckin' kid."

"And I'll tell nana you swore," Matty yelled after him.

Jerry gave him the finger and kept going.

That was the end of Jerry and my wank sessions because Matty shadowed us each and every one of the three days that remained of our school break. In a way, I was glad because I'm not sure Jerry would have appreciated my hands-on approach had I plucked up the courage to help him out.

Once Jerry left I had only myself to practice manual labor on, testing various hand movements to get the best sensations. By the time he returned I knew my technique was magic and there was no way I'd keep my hands off his very appealing cock. He wouldn't want me to. The weather had a very different idea. It was the beginning of one of the coldest and blusteriest summers on record. On the beach, the sand whipped up by the wind blasted against our legs and arms and face like a phalanx of pins, making any excursion into the hills a painful exercise. We abandoned plans to trek to our hideaway in the dunes after a few minutes in the melee of projectile sand.

I had to promise Matt – he had asked me not to call him Matty any longer as it sounded too childlike – I would spend quality time with him on this break and, as if to further thwart my plans to get a hold of Jerry's dick, I heard Mrs. Fitton arguing in the backyard with Jerry. "There's to be no running off and leaving your brother behind this time, do you understand?"

Jerry grumbled.

"I mean it," she said.

It pelted with unseasonable rain. We were lucky that my nan had a fibro cabin at the back of the property. It had served as makeshift accommodation when my parents were alive. I used to 'sleep out' in the cabin while mum and dad took the second bedroom inside the house. The cabin was still set up although apart from the beds there had been a tendency to shove any old thing in when there was nowhere else to put it. I had the great idea of playing some sort of war game where two of us (preferably me and Jerry) hid under one bed while Matt hid under another. In retrospect, the game seems nonsensical but all three of us jumped at the idea – that's how bored we were.

There was a rule that the solo soldier had to sneak up on the others but if we heard him approach he had to take a five-minute time out and go back to his 'base' under the other bed. Jerry and I discovered we could manage a good wank, especially if one of us kept his eye out for Matt's approach. That, however, made it difficult for that person to play with his cock. There was method in my madness suggesting it.

"I've got an idea, Jerry. You get your dick out and then lie on your side to watch out for Matty. Okay?"

He seemed nervous.

"Trust me," I smiled. "You'll enjoy it."

He struggled out of his shorts, his cock already hard as steel, and peeked from the blankets hanging over the side of the bed which provided cover for our activity. I squeezed some baby oil onto my palm – I now had my own supply that I'd purchased with my pocket money and kept hidden – warming it up before I put my hand around Jerry's cock. He flinched. Before he could tell me to cut it out, I began to stroke him, using every trick that I'd learned from experimenting on my own cock.

He ducked his head back to watch me. "Shit, that feels good," he whispered. "You've been practicing."

I kept right on pleasuring him and, in no time at all, he blew a load into the old towel I kept handy for our games. He shucked up his shorts and I went to take his place on watch, lowering mine as I wriggled into position. He looked dubious about touching my prick. He ran his fingers along the shaft, his touch gossamer-like when what I wanted was a firm grip. I'd fondled his balls as well as jerking him off and what he was doing no how fitted my idea of reciprocal behavior.

"For fuck's sake, grab it and wank me," I whispered, desperate to blow a load.

"When did you get such a potty mouth?" he chuckled.

At least it broke the ice. He dribbled oil into his hand and wrapped it around my cock, sliding up and down much less firmly than I did on his. His technique was tentative at best but at least Jerry was touching me. It was another step forward although I had no idea at that stage where these steps were taking us.

We both came twice that day although Matt got very impatient with the game, so that on the second day, the wind still lashing against the window as Jerry and I were snug under the bed, he insisted I was his partner and that Jerry be the soldier to attack us. I left Jerry the oil and the towel and from the hiccupped little groans from his position, I assumed he was putting them to good use. Matt, on the other hand, came armed with a pile of comics and a flashlight. Immersed in his world of superheroes and nasty villains, he kept himself amused for hours, occasionally calling my attention to something that particularly took his fancy in his reading material. Eventually, he fell asleep and I took the opportunity to scramble under the other bed with Jerry where I had an opportunity to help him out with his second ejaculation of the day. He wasn't inclined to help me out when I wiggled my erection in his direction.

At the end of the summer break he was still as reticent as ever. I'd have to help him overcome that next summer. As it turned out he didn't clasp his hand around my dick then, either, because he was in hospital with appendicitis and wouldn't be at his grandparents place again until the following year. Damn.

I spent my free time with Matt who was more like a puppy than a human. He followed me everywhere which was not as irritating as it sounds. Without Jerry, I had little to do and Matt's wild-eyed enthusiasm for everything I suggested was an endearing quality to someone who bored as easily as I did. I learned in the fortnight we spent in each other's company, me playing big brother, that Matt was probably a nicer version of Jerry. He was funny, intelligent, eager for new experiences. He jumped at the opportunity when I suggested we go fishing off the bridge.

We sat side by side dangling our lines in the clear greeny-blue water, watching large fish circle the bread on the end of the hooks. Conversation was easy and that summer I learned a lot about Matt although I knew most of it was a young boy's preoccupations and they would change as he grew to maturity.

"Hey, that fish grabbed the bait," he said. "What do I do now?"

I was envious. I'd never managed to snare anything but a rubber bicycle tire in all the years I'd been fishing. "Reel him in carefully. That's it. Wind the line around the spool. Careful. That's it. You got him."

The fish was a beauty. It would make a good meal at the Fittons that night. It put up a good fight, flopping about on the end of the line, the hook embedded in its mouth.

Matt's lip quivered.

"What's the matter?" I asked.

"I don't want it. Look, it's in pain."

"I don't think fish feel pain like we do," I replied to calm him down.

Matt was becoming more and more distressed. "Put it back in the water."

"Okay, Matt. Take it easy, mate. Give me your line. I have to take the hook out of his mouth." If only the fish had been more co-operative, it would have saved time and resulted in less damage to its mouth, but it insisted on flapping about like it was suffocating. I didn't dare tell Matt it was. Eventually, I managed to extract the savage hook. I held the fish out to Matt who gave it his blessing by patting its flank, whispering, "Be free" before I tossed it back into the lake. That was the end of our fishing expedition.

Instead, I took him to one of the fish and chip shops in the town center where we got a big serve of chips smothered in vinegar and salt, wrapped in white butcher's paper. We sat at a picnic table where Matt managed to feed most of his share to marauding seagulls once I'd warned him to break the chips in half and let them cool before he offered them. It was a pleasant way to spend the afternoon.

I asked him about school because he'd let slip he wasn't enjoying it. "What's the problem?" I enquired.

For a change, he was remarkably reluctant to talk about it, but with a bit of cajoling he admitted he'd been bullied through most of the previous year.

"Sounds like what happened to me when I first came to Lakesmouth," I told him.

"What did you do?"

"Well, I was much younger than you and I went home crying a lot. They tried to break me, but I just ignored it. It was mainly name calling, never anything physical. What about yours?"

"Mainly spitting and swearing and calling me names."

"Like what."

"Faggot." he sniffed.

"Have you told Jerry?"

"Hell, no. That would just make it worse."

"What about a teacher or your parents?"

He sighed. I was no help at all.

"You could always try humor. Ask him how he knows you're a faggot when you haven't sucked his dick."

Matt almost choked on the chip he had in his mouth and I had to pound him on the back and hand him his can of soft drink. His eyes were filled with tears of surprise and delight, even as he puked up his half-digested lunch. "Sorry, mate," I said.

"See," he gasped. "That's why I think you're great. You don't talk down to me like everyone else. You treat me like…" he looked at me as if he was too frightened to go on.

"Like what?"

I heard him gulp. "Like I matter."

The next summer things changed. Jerry changed. He brought a friend from school with him and they had surf boards. Jerry had grown into a strapping teenager, blond wisps of hair on his chin and upper lip. He strutted about the town in just his board shorts, his tanned body not exactly rippling with muscle but he had a lot better definition that I did. He avoided me as much as possible although Matt filled the gap. In fact, he came charging into nan's place not long after his parents had deposited him and Jerry, and Jerry's new friend, Simon, at the Fittons'.

"Hey, Sam," he yelled through the back screen door until I came out to greet him. He was bobbing excitedly on the balls of his feet. He was excited. "It worked. It bloody worked." He looked around to make sure no one had heard him swearing.

I smiled at his enthusiasm although I had no idea what he was talking about. I had to ask.

He lowered his voice. "What you told me to do about the bully."

I had a faint recollection we'd discussed it once. "What did you do?"

"Every time he called me 'faggot,' I asked how he knew when I hadn't sucked his dick yet. His mates laughed but that just made him angrier. He kept right on calling me names so I taunted him by saying, 'You seem awfully obsessed with my sex life' – not that I have one – 'so if you want to make a date, just call me'." He did that cute thing with his thumb and little finger miming a phone, minced provocatively, and winked. I laughed despite myself.

"How did he take that?"

"Not well. His friends had to drag him off me before he could throw a punch. But, you know what? I felt him. He was hard in his pants when he pushed me up against the wall. So every time I saw him in the school grounds or in the hallway, I'd look all shy and call out so everyone heard, 'Why haven't you called me? I thought you wanted me'."

"That was very brave."

"Nah. I just did what you said. I kept it up for a few weeks until he was cracking up and he finally came to me and begged me to stop harassing him."

"You harassing him?"

"Yeah. I told him that now he knew what it was like to be bullied. I told him if he ever tried to make my life hell again, I would make his life so miserable he'd be the laughing stock of the entire school."

I clapped him on the back in admiration. "Good for you."

He got shy on me. "Um…you want to spend some time with me this holiday?"

"Sure," I said. "Doesn't look like Jerry has any time for me."

"He's an asshole."

Asshole or not, I still fancied Jerry like a straight guy would fancy a girl.

I attempted to make contact with Jerry, and Simon, but they seemed to spend every waking moment on their boards. Even Matt seemed to be seduced by the waves that summer and I heard Jerry encourage him to spend more time in the fresh air. "It's much healthier than being cooped up all day with that…with Sam next door. A helluva lot healthier."

"You used to spend a lot of time with him up until now," Matt replied.

"Yeah, and that's why I'm telling you it's healthier to keep him at arm's length."

Whether Matt believed his brother that I was an unsavory character or not, he did keep pretty much to himself until the final week of the holidays when he knocked on the back door to see if I was home. We sat on the back step to chat.

"Sorry, I haven't been around much," he said, "but I've been working on something. I'd like it if you could come and see. Tomorrow. Near the surf club on the beach on the other side of the bridge."

"Sure. What time.?"

"Around two."

I was curious as to his secret but before I could question him any further, Jerry popped his head over the fence separating the two properties. "What the fuck are you doing in there?" he demanded.

"Talking to Sam. What it look like?"

"Don't cheek me, you little brat."

"Then mind your own business."

"You are my business, little brother."

"Not so little any more. I'm catching up to you. Fast."

"I warned you about going in there. Now get your ass back inside before I teach you a lesson."

"You don't own me."

I decided to broker a peace. "Off you go, Matt. I'll see you later."

"Okay. Remember we got a date."

I saw the look of disgust on Jerry's face at the word 'date.' I knew he'd totally misunderstood and that Matt was in for a heap of abuse. It began once Matt had gone back to his grandparents' house and continued with much shouting and slamming of doors until Matt ran out the back screaming, "Stop treating me like a little kid."

The next day I almost reconsidered going to meet Matt. I didn't want to be the wedge between the two brothers, not that they'd ever really got along. I decided I wasn't going to be intimidated by Jerry. I didn't know what his trouble was but I guessed he had a load of guilt about our jerk-off sessions.

When I reached the Lakesmouth Surf Club, it was set up for a competition. I looked around for Matt but he wasn't in the crowd that sat on the sand behind the tape and flags that marked the spectator area. Then I noticed him with a group of teenagers near a marshal's desk. He had a large number '5' painted on the side of his leg. I couldn't believe it – he was obviously part of the competition. I looked around for Jerry and the Fittons but they were nowhere to be seen. I felt strangely elated that he'd invited me to attend but that his family either hadn't bothered or were ignorant of his pursuits.

The announcement over the makeshift PA revealed the next heat was the Under-15s. Matt looked around the crowd and saw me, his face lighting up like a Christmas tree. He nodded at me and I nodded back, proud to be part of a secret ritual. Matt had turned into a really special kid.

Just how special became apparent as the heat progressed. I knew he hadn't been on a board until quite recently but he placed a very creditable fifth, even though there was quite a points gap between him and the teenager who placed fourth. Matt waited until after the presentation, applauding generously for the winners before he made his way over to where I waited.

"You were so good," I gushed.

"Thanks. It meant a lot to have you here."

"What about your family?"

He shrugged. "The oldies don't consider surfboard riding a real sport and Jerry is off somewhere with Simon." The way he screwed up his nose on Simon's name meant there was history between the two of them but I'd let my questions lie for the moment.

"You want to go grab a bite to eat?"

"Oh, man. I wish I could but I gotta hang round here to suck up to the important dudes. Can I take a rain check?"

"Of course you can."

I don't know why, but I was disappointed.

Later that afternoon as I was reading one of the novels assigned for the following school year, I heard more arguments from the Fittons' house. It was so loud it brought my grandmother out into the living room where I had the book propped up on the coffee table while I sat on the carpet.

"What on earth is going on next door?" she asked. "They've been going on like that for days. They sound like animals."

"Jerry and Matt have never particularly liked each other," I said, hoping my name wouldn't come up in their argument because nan would want to know why.

"You better go in there and tell them to quieten down otherwise they'll have the police on their doorstep."

"I don't want to get involved."

She looked at me suspiciously. "Have you fallen out with Jerry?"

"Not really," I replied. "He's just spending all his time with that Simon friend of his. They go to school together."

"Can't say I'm sorry. I've heard the sort of language he uses when he thinks no one is listening. He's a bad influence if ever there was one."

She tutted to herself as she went back to the small sewing room where she did a bit of mending while listening to her old Bakelite radio. I went back to my book, keeping one ear out for what was being shouted just across the back fence.

Matt came in the say a quick goodbye the morning he and Jerry were being picked up by their parents. "Thanks for everything. Hope we can catch up next holidays. Here's my phone number," he said, thrusting a piece of paper into my hands. "Give me a call if you get a chance."

His mum called his name and he had to go. He hugged me warmly, something he'd never done before. "See ya," he said and disappeared.

It was in the weeks that followed that I met Rory.

I would have been eager to share my experiences with Jerry the next time he turned up to visit his grandparents but he was again tagged by the inscrutable Simon who never seemed to leave his side. Even Matt was more downbeat than usual although he did find time to catch me in private to tell me, "I've been warned off spending time with you."

"In god's name, why?"

"No one will say, except that a friendship between the two of us is considered unhealthy."

I knew what they were getting at, but it had to be of Jerry's doing. Bastard. I had designs on him, not his little brother.

"For your own sake then, you better not let them catch you talking to me."

He laughed. "You should know by now I don't take any notice of what people tell me to do."

"Yeah. You sure are a contrary little bastard."

"Hey. Enough of the little. I'm almost as big as you now."

He'd really put on a growth spurt in the last year. He'd also bulked up. He was going to be a heartbreaker when he got older. He took after Jerry in that respect.

I must have said something along those lines out loud because he looked at me with a nervous grin.

"I'll be catching waves around the surf club if you're ever in the vicinity. You never know, we might accidentally run into each other. Talk over old times."

"Yeah. It's a free country."

"I hope to see ya, Sam. It's not the same without a good friend."

I left it a couple of days before I ventured across the bridge to the surf club. I changed into my Speedos and lay on my striped beach towel to soak up the rays. I couldn't see Matt out among the breakers or anywhere on the beach. The warmth of the sun lolled me into snoozing from which I was awakened rudely by seawater dripping on my face and chest. It was bloody cold.

I sat up quickly. "What the…"

Matt shook his head, his blond locks spraying water like a dog attempting to dry itself off. "You bastard," I yelled, although he knew I said it in jest. He'd already laid his board on the sand so I tackled him, throwing him off balance, sitting on his chest to hold him down. He shucked me off easily, forcing me onto my back in the sand, pressing me down with his body, his arms on either side of my head meant he was looking me straight in the eyes. I shivered at what I read in his. Before I could beg him to get off me because he was much stronger than I was, he leaned down and brushed his lips over mine, pushing his tongue into my mouth. I was so surprised I opened my mouth to suggest it wasn't a good idea but he choked off any objection I was about to make.

The kiss didn't last long. I just prayed that anyone who witnessed it would perhaps mistake it for mouth-to-mouth resuscitation. Matt pulled away from me. He was smiling. "I've wanted to do that for such a long time."

I was panting. "Whoa, Matt. Who taught you to kiss like that?"

"That was my first kiss," he boasted.

"You should give lessons. You're a natural."

"Nah. I can only do it with people I like."

Before we could discuss it any further, I heard Jerry's voice boom across the sand. "What the fuck are you doing?"

Matt didn't seem perturbed by the interruption; he sat back on his haunches, sneering at his brother. "What's it look like I'm doing? Crocheting mittens?"

"Watch your mouth, little brother."

"Oh, I will. I have no intention of putting it in the same place you put yours."

I saw the spark of anger in Jerry's eyes. "Leave it, Matt," I whispered.

He stood up, allowing me to scramble to my feet.

Jerry turned his attention to me. "I told you to keep your filthy hands off my brother."

"In case you're interested, big brother, it was me had his hands all over Sam."

Jerry, of course, was the distraction. It wasn't until I felt the thump against the back of my skull, I realized Simon had been creeping up behind us. I heard a gasp from Matt as I went down. When I regained consciousness, a crowd had gathered around me and one of the surf lifesavers from the club was speaking to me, holding two fingers in front of my face asking me how many. I answered the usual questions about the date, the prime minister, and other trivialities before he helped me into the clubhouse where he offered to call a cab to take me to the hospital.

I'd taken the opportunity to look around but there was no sign of Matt, Jerry or Simon. I declined the offer of a hospital visit, swearing I had no idea who'd clobbered me from behind, but before he would let me go, the lifesaver reinforced the possibility of concussion and what to watch out for. After promising to follow his instructions to the letter if I became nauseous, he allowed me to leave. I staggered a little at first until I got my balance, then made my way back toward the center of town, keen to get away from the people who had witnessed my humiliation. I made myself sit quietly in a café where I had a warm milky tea and raisin toast which was in no danger of being regurgitated.

I eventually made my way home, collapsing on my bed and sleeping away most of the day. I was awoken by the sounds of arguing and the slamming of car doors before engines turned over and they drove away. I could guess what has happened and the following day the Fittons' house seemed strangely deserted. I had a headache, nothing serious, just bad enough to make life miserable. I took two aspirin telling nan I was feeling unwell. She was about to get out the warm brandy until I told her it was just a headache. She left me alone for the remainder of the day, just bringing a thick broth to my bedside later in the evening.

I wasn't hungry. I was angry. I was surprised. I was…I didn't know what I was. Except confused.

A couple of days went by before my head was clear enough to formulate a plan. I had to find out what Matt meant by the kiss. I'd never given him any encouragement. Hell, I didn't even know he was queer. I found his phone number on the slip of paper pushed to the back of one of my drawers. I needed to ring long distance and the best place to do that was not from the public phone box at the end of the street, but over at the post office in the center of town. It had a bank of booths that gave a certain amount of privacy and which meant you were not in as much danger of an impatient caller banging on the glass in an effort to get you to hurry up.

I had to wait a few minutes for a booth to become available during which I noticed something peculiar. The post office had pride of place just to the side of the park in which the carnival set up tents in summer. Directly over the road were the main Lakesmouth shops, one of which was the local farmers' co-op which sold fresh fruit and vegetables from the farms that dotted the area.

On my way back home late at night I'd often noticed the 'young farmer', as my nan called him, who worked diligently stocking up and rearranging the produce. He usually worked stripped to the waist, wearing nothing but a pair of tight shorts that left little to the imagination. His ass was muscular, and he displayed quite a bulge in the front. He was a good deal older than me. With my new awareness of things sexual, I took a closer look at him while I waited for a phone booth to become available. It would have been too suspicious to stop at the glass doors and stare in, but from the opposite side of the street I could stare unobserved for as long as I wanted. He had the lights blazing in the shop so it was easy to see him. He kept gazing out the glass frontage as if searching for something.

A number of cars stopped close by. It was understandable; there was a toilet block nearby and most of the men who used the facilities were probably on their way home from the pub. While I watched, a number of men entered the urinal at different times and when they emerged, the lights under the co-op's awning above the footpath flickered. At first I thought the lights were faulty until I watched more closely and saw the farmer flick the switch each time a good-looking man emerged from the gents.

I was intrigued but a booth became available and I didn't want to miss the opportunity to talk to Matt. Nervously I waited for the operator who told me how many coins to deposit in the black metal contraption and then I waited. The phone rang at the other end and I heard someone answer. The operator told me to 'Press Button A' and I was through. "Um, is Matt there?" I asked.

"Who is this?" a woman asked. I guessed it was Matt's mother. "It's Sam from Lakesmouth," I said. Probably not the smartest thing to identify myself.

When she said "Oh," it was cold enough to freeze water, and I knew I'd have little chance of speaking to Matt. "He's out," she said, before adding acidly, "With his girlfriend." She hung up the phone before I had a chance to ask her to inform him I'd called.

My stomach felt like it was full of concrete. I stumbled out of the phone booth, tears threatening to overwhelm me, but I kept myself in check long enough to walk over to one of the picnic tables and sit staring miserably into space. I'd try again tomorrow and keep trying until Matt answered the phone. Once I'd formulated a plan, I felt better. I realized I was looking at the co-op and that the farmer was flicking the outside light yet again. As I watched, a middle-aged man walked across the street to tap on the glass shop front. The farmer let him inside and there seemed to be a certain amount of intimate touching before they looked around anxiously to see if anyone had caught them. I was sufficiently hidden in the dark that there was little chance they would catch me spying.

Shortly after, the light inside the co-op went out. *Must be the farmer's friend, ready to drive him home,* I thought to myself. I played the past few days over and over in my mind looking for clues but remained as confused as ever. It must have been about half an hour later that my ruminations were interrupted by the lights in the co-op flickering back on.

The middle-aged visitor was adjusting his trousers as he exited the shop and hurried across the road to his car. The young farmer went back to his work. I headed home.

The next night was much the same as the first, although once I heard Matt's mother answer the phone I knew I was letting myself in for more humiliation if I persevered. I hung up, preferring to watch the shenanigans as another man crossed the road to the fruit and veg emporium after the farmer had flicked the lights. I waited patiently until the visitor came out about forty minutes later. I think it was the humor of the situation that kept me from totally falling apart.

The third night I skipped phoning and spent my time lurking in the shadows watching the intricate sex play occurring in front of people's noses. No one else seemed to notice a steady stream of men making their way to the co-op where, once inside, the lights would go out, only to be switched on again when the visitor left usually about thirty to forty-five minutes later. Some nights he had one guest, on the odd occasion, he had multiple partners.

I got into the habit of varying the times I called Matt's number but always with the same result. It was about a fortnight after the first call that I realized I was being stupid. There are only so many times you can beat your head against a wall before it finally knocks some sense into you. Swearing it was the last time I'd make the call, I asked the operator for the number. I'm surprised we weren't on first-name terms by then. I recognized Jerry's voice this time. "Stop fucking calling. We know it's you, Sam. If you call again, we'll go to the police."

I hung up.

I was angry that I had wasted so much time on the Cliffords. They were assholes. It was time to get my life back.

The lights in the co-op were blazing and the farmer was displaying his body as if he were a living mannequin in a shop window. It was early yet and there were no cars in the vicinity. I strode across the street and stood with my back to the shop as if I were waiting for someone, glancing at my watch and then gazing up the main street. Affecting the look of an exasperated boyfriend, I paced up and down the footpath, giving me the opportunity to see what the farmer was up to. He appeared tense at my encroachment on his territory because a number of vehicles were now parked outside the men's toilet. No way was I going to relinquish my spot.

He didn't take the hint, so I had to improvise. Removing my watch, I glanced one more time up the street looking for my phantom date, shrugged with resignation and then, heart beating wildly at the audacity of my next move, I knocked on the glass shop front. The farmer seemed exasperated as he opened the door.

"Can I help you?" he asked politely.

"I was wondering if you could tell me the time?"

He smirked. "What? It's too difficult to take your watch out of your pocket to see for yourself?"

"Snap," I replied.

"What do you really want?"

"Can I come in for a moment?"

He stood aside and I entered the shop.

"Now, what can I do for you?"

"For the past two weeks I've been watching you from over near the post office…"

"Shit. Are you a cop?"

I was quick to assuage his concerns. "Nah. Just an interested onlooker."

His smile returned. "How interested?"

"Why don't you turn the light out and see?"

He looked me up and down. "I usually prefer them a bit older but you're a pretty young thing. How old are you?"

"Nineteen."

"Had much experience?"

There was no point in lying. "I was hoping you could help me out."

He grabbed my hand, switched off the light, and led me through the back of the shop to what appeared to be a storeroom which was set up for the sorts of assignations in which he was obviously involved.

"Take your clothes off," he said making it plain this quick liaison would be all physical with no emotional component. That was okay, I needed someone to teach me what to do. In the end, I could not have chosen a better teacher. Ted, as the young farmer turned out to be named, was indeed a farmer as well as a skilled sexual athlete. Our first meeting saw me face down over a rough wooden crate of some vegetable I couldn't identify in the semi-darkness, Ted's cock wedged in my liberally greased ass, as he fucked me senseless. It took a while to get accustomed to having his quite substantial prick in my butt – I would have preferred at least a modicum of foreplay, not that I knew what that involved – but Ted seemed the sort of man who liked to get to the crux of the matter right away. I assume he wanted to get back to his fruit stacking as soon as possible.

He must have tagged my ass for about ten minutes before he let fly with a burst of expletives, held my waist tightly, his cock exploding in my ass. It wasn't quite "Is that all there is?" but it wasn't far from it. Ted pulled out and I felt some of his cum dribble down my leg. After he'd carefully wiped his prick on an old towel, he tossed it to me to clean up. I'm afraid I lost it.

"Is that it?" I squealed. "You fuck me in less than half the time you take on the other men you invite back here, and give me a dirty old towel to wipe up. Fuck, I haven't even come yet."

"You are a feisty one." He pushed me against a bale of newspapers and I sat uncomfortably, not having bothered to pull up my trousers as yet. Kneeling between my legs he licked my balls as he stroked my cock, now oozing with excitement. I didn't want to come too quickly. Even though this was more a learning exercise for me than it was relief, if I was lucky, relief would be a very pleasurable by-product. I took note of the way in which he used his tongue and his lips, the way his fingers caressed my sac before he ran his hands across my nipples, pinching then slightly which made my entire body shudder. Nipples? Who knew?

"You've got a nice big cock," he mumbled as he lifted it between his lips. "I'd like to feel that up my ass one day."

"Just tell me when," I gasped as he engulfed my entire prick in his warm mouth. I felt his throat close around the head and a couple of inches and wondered how the fuck he did that without choking. He was more of an expert than Rory. I still didn't get my full thirty minutes because, all too soon, I blew my load down his thirsty throat.

He patted my exhausted cock as he stood up, brushing his knees, before telling me to take my time, and exited back into the shop. It took me a few minutes to find the towel to wipe myself, and to recover from the intensity of the experience. When I finally joined him, he looked into my eyes as if attempting to read my soul. He reached up to push a few loose strands of hair back behind my ear. "You'll be a real heartbreaker once you get a bit more experience. But you can't just lie there, you know, as some bloke is plugging your ass. There's more to it than that."

"Teach me then."

He went back to the task of stocking the shelves and I settled into a rhythm helping him out.

"I don't want you cramping my style," he said.

"Okay."

"I don't do relationships."

"Okay."

"I have regulars. I suppose I could take on another one for variety."

"I can help around the shop," I said in order to show how eager I was.

For the next few months, until I headed to the city to get my teaching degree, Ted took great pains to teach me as best he could. I helped out at night as we chatted about our lives and he gave me advice on places to go in the city and how to avoid the cops. When he saw someone he liked at the beat across the road, I would disappear until he had his 'client' ensconced in the back. I'd go back to work stacking boxes or other chores he trusted me with. Later, he'd allow me to fuck him across the same boxes on which he'd taken my virginity.

I told nan where I was working evenings. She was not impressed. Her initial reluctance to allow it to continue, as she believed I was being taken advantage of, was overcome when Ted began his charm offensive on the very next occasion she visited the shop for her weekly green groceries and he threw in a couple of complimentary mangos or cantaloupes or something that was almost too ripe to sell any more. She could see that I enjoyed the work and eventually gave her blessing, "That farmer Ted is a fine cut of a man. You could do worse than be like him."

That's what I'm trying to do, Nan. Be like him.

Eventually, I was skilled enough that Ted allowed me to join him and a stranger to make up a threesome, and I began to get frisky, flicking the light to attract my own partners while Ted was busy. I'm surprised the local authorities never cottoned on to what we were doing. It was with real regret I left Lakesmouth to attend university, but if I was to have a career, it wouldn't be in this backwater. I spent my final night plowing Ted into the floor of his storeroom. I made it as rough and tumble as I could because he appreciated it more than something schmaltzy and sentimental.

He kissed me on the cheek as we said our goodbyes and I noticed a small tear in the corner of his eye.

"I'll be back again at Christmas. I'll pop in and see you then," I assured him.

"You take good care of yourself, young Sam."

"I owe you a great deal, Ted."

"Go on, you're a natural. Now piss off, I've got work to do. This fruit won't stack itself."

I let myself out while he had his back turned. I didn't want an emotional farewell either. I stood farther along the street for a moment to engrave the shop in my memory. I smiled when, less than five minutes after my departure, I noticed the co-op lights flicker to signal an older man in a beige Holden parked near the post office. You had to love Ted.

I never did see Ted again. My grandmother wrote to me about six months later to tell me he was dead. He'd been found in the co-op lying in a pool of blood. Someone had bashed him to death. The cops believed it was a robbery gone wrong, and no one was going to correct them. His murder went unsolved. The next summer when I was back in Lakesmouth, I went to the cemetery to place flowers on his grave. I owed a lot to Ted and I would miss him. His advice had proved as invaluable as his lessons in sexual calisthenics.

I furthered my lessons in the city, far enough from nan's all-encompassing morality that she would never discover my transgressions. Because I could never go back to my old life, I remained in the city after I graduated, getting a job as a high school English and History teacher in one of the depressed inner-city suburbs. Nan had her heart set on me moving back with her but she understood I had my own life to live although she pestered me for great grandchildren.

When the doctor rang me about her cancer I knew my obligation was to the woman who had raised me. I pleaded my case with the Education Department knowing full well it was difficult to get a placement in a coastal area like Lakesmouth. It was a prime location, but I was fortunate that the little wooden school where I'd spent many a miserable year had been demolished, the pampas grass cleared, and a modern primary and secondary school built to accommodate the burgeoning population. I walked into a position on the say-so of a sympathetic bureaucrat whose mother had recently succumbed to terminal illness.

Eight years after I left Lakesmouth, I was back again. I had little time for a private life in the two years

I watched nan deteriorate. The pain made her grumpy and unpleasant and many's the time I thought about putting her into care. She was adamant she wanted to die at home, even though the doctors maintained she would have more comfort in a hospice. "No, thank you, I want to die in my own bed," she would tell them irascibly, shaking the stick she used now to support her as she limped to the toilet. She couldn't stand to use a pot.

She was buried, as requested. "You're not going to burn me. If you even contemplate it for a second, I'll come back and make your life a misery," she said one day when I suggested cremation. She's a couple of rows down from Ted and, on the odd occasion I go to talk to nan, or ask her advice, I drop by Ted to laugh over old times.

"I HEAR your granny died," Jerry said, his voice dripping with spite. "What was it killed her? She die of shame?"

I wanted to hit the bastard, but I was outnumbered by at least twenty to one. Besides, I wanted information. "How's Matt? What's he up to these days?"

Jerry's voice dripped vitriol. "None of your fuckin' business."

"Fuck off, faggot," the girl beside him hissed belligerently.

The atmosphere at the party was tense, I didn't want to provoke them. I turned to go.

"By the way," Jerry said. "Don't cry like a sissy but you won't see me again. The house has been sold. Some rich dick who runs a surfboard design factory. Don't think it hasn't been…"

I didn't hear any more. I was out the door and half way across the yard when I heard the raucous laughter, obviously at my expense. I went inside, locked the door, closed the windows, and pulled down the blinds. That part of my life was now history.

About a month later, a van emblazoned with the logo of a surfboard company that even I, in my ignorance, had heard of was parked in the front yard of the Fittons' old place when I got back home from my teaching job. There had been intermittent activity in the house over the weeks with builders patching up parts of the home that had fallen into disrepair, a large shed erected in the back yard, and various other improvements that inevitably made my home look shabby by comparison.

It spurred me to make up my mind about my future as I'd procrastinated about making a decision. Sure, I liked living in Lakesmouth. It had become more cosmopolitan in outlook but it still lacked the sort of night-time attractions that would make my life more pleasurable. I couldn't see me settling into middle-age still attempting to pick up tourists in the summer. I wanted a partner to share my life with. The only place I would find that was in the city.

The Teaching Positions Vacant sat open on the dining-room table. I'd ringed a couple of possibilities but it was daunting that I would have to pack up and move, as well as search for new accommodation. It was too soon after nan's death. I needed more time to adjust. Still, it wouldn't hurt to just see what was on offer. A loud explosion of cackles burst from the backyard followed by the barking of what sounded like the Hound of the Baskervilles. I jumped up and ran outside almost colliding with someone who appeared down the side of the house whistling for the bloody dog that was playing havoc with the chooks.

"What the fuck?" the intruder swore, just managing to avoid knocking me down. He was a big bastard. Obviously a surfer if his tan and his yellow blond hair were anything to go by. He was fit, too. His muscles made my mouth water. Handsome as…fuck!

"Come here, Oscar," he called to the collie who declined to take any notice of him.

"Matty?"

He seemed to stop breathing, turning toward me slowly, staring as if he didn't believe his eyes. "Sammy?"

I couldn't help it, I hugged him. It's what you do when you meet a long-lost friend.

We both started talking at once. Then we both stopped.

"You never rang." His tone was accusatory.

"Your mother said you wouldn't take my calls."

He smiled. "I didn't know."

"You want…you know…um…a coffee?" I was suddenly tongue-tied.

"Sure. Why not?"

He called the dog who came obediently this time having scared the chooks half to death. "This is Oscar."

I scratched the dog behind the ears making me his instant friend.

"So, you still live here?" Matt asked.

"I moved back when nan got sick."

"Oh?"

"She passed away a few weeks back. Cancer."

"Oh, I am sorry," he said, putting his hand on my shoulder in an expression of sympathy.

We sat on my ratty old lounge, attempting to crowd too much information into too little time, both avoiding the really personal, preferring to sketch our lives in broad strokes. I told him the basics of my becoming a teacher and he revealed he ran his own business designing and building customized surf boards. He seemed pleased when I whistled and told him I'd heard of his company name.

Glancing at his watch, he apologized profusely. "Look, I have an important business meeting in half an hour. I'd really like to catch up some more. How about dinner some time?"

"Sure."

"When are you free?"

"Just about any night."

"Great," he enthused. "How about…tonight?"

I shrugged. "I'm not doing anything."

"I should be finished with the accountants by six. How about I come pick you up about seven?"

"Fine by me."

"Dress casual."

After Matt left, I don't know why I had butterflies in my stomach. Perhaps it was the fact he'd grown into a gorgeous hunk of man. Okay, that was my dick talking – Matt was more than a lump of meat. Maybe we could salvage a friendship from the ashes of our boyhood. Still, I didn't know in what direction his sexual proclivities lay. And there was also the mystery of what had happened on that fateful day when he kissed me, and its aftermath. Obviously, something had gone very right for him.

I must have changed outfits four or five times. Was it stupid of me wanting to impress? Matt had seen me at my slovenly best when he'd caught me attempting to round up his dog, so it was important I look as dazzling as possible this time. I was deaf to the little spark of conscience that told me the only reason I wanted to dazzle was because I wanted him in my bed. Consciences can be such a bore – especially when they're right.

I suppose my weeks with Ted and my peripatetic sexual life didn't have me contemplating anything long-term with Matt. Hell, I didn't even know if he was gay. Jerry's teenage same-sex exploration had obviously been hormone-driven and he'd settled for 'normalcy' over time. Matt's fumbled kiss, though, I believed was something different. Oh well, no use agonizing over it at that moment, I'd had ten years of doing that. Tonight at dinner, with any luck, I'd know the truth.

Of course, I didn't. Have dinner with Matt, that is. I'd dressed up to no avail. He was a no show. I wasn't surprised really. The kiss loomed large in my memory while, I suspect, Matt didn't even remember it, although there had to be some reason for the warmth in his greeting at seeing me after so long. Wishful thinking? Much.

He'd probably thought better of rekindling memories of a painful past. I wouldn't blame him. It had been humiliating for me to meet Jerry again although I now questioned why I had found him so attractive as a teenager when he'd grown into a homophobic asshole. Guilt? Was he sublimating a desire to have me touch his cock again? I really doubted that. Besides, I didn't care. I had more pride than to waste my time with such a repellent character.

What's to say Matt wasn't like his brother? Why didn't Jerry tell me that Matt had bought the house? Or was he merely renovating it to sell? My mind was a swirl of questions not the least of which was: *where the fuck are you, Matt?*

I'd changed out of my clothes meant-to-impress into old-and-comfortable to zap a quick meal – microwaved frozen spinach and ricotta cannelloni with a small rocket and sun-dried tomato salad. So shoot me, I'm lazy, and not the world's best cook. I should then have begun marking my students' school assignments but I was strangely agitated and found it difficult to concentrate, so much so that it wasn't until the head detective on some crime series on the TV unmasked the killer that I realized I had no idea what the plot was.

Meeting Matt again had knocked the wind out of me. It had been a rocky few months what with nan passing away, meeting Jerry again, and now Matt turning up as the owner of the house next door.

I thought the best place for me was bed. I'd sleep the anxiety out of me. Reading was a natural soporific but the words seemed to be a jumbled mess, impenetrable to my mind, so I put the book aside and leaned to turn off the reading lamp when there was loud knocking at the door.

Shit! It was not unusual for people to get lost in Lakesmouth North, believing there was a through-road to the lighthouse and townships to the north. But there wasn't. You had to drive all the way around the lake to get to a point that was a matter of five or six miles from my house. Bloody ridiculous, but there you go. Strangers never believed it until a local swore it was the way it is. I guess I was the only one with a light on, thus the reason for the knock. I was already wearing an old T-shirt that had seen better days, so I tugged on a pair of sweatpants to answer. Whoever it was began rapping their knuckles against the wooden door impatiently as I began unbolting it.

I was surprised when Matt burst into the house, pushing me aside as he apologized profusely. "I'm so sorry, I don't know what you must think of me. You must have thought I'd had second thoughts about seeing you again. Or else I was a prick tease."

Prick tease?

The words tumbled out of his mouth in such quick succession they became garbled.

He took a quick breath. "I guess what I'm trying to say is—" Grabbing my face, he planted a kiss against my mouth. Well, that answered one question. I parted my lips to give him access and from the moan he stifled, I thought he appreciated it. Our tongues battled it out for supremacy but it was good-natured. When he drew back to catch his breath, he saw my smile.

"So, Matt, no wife?" I asked.

"Uh uh."

"Girlfriend?"

"Uh uh."

"Boyfriend?"

"No attachments whatsoever. Except to Oscar."

Bloody dog was getting all the affection I wanted.

He seemed almost afraid to ask the next question. "What about you?"

"Ditto."

His face broke out into the broadest smile I'd ever seen. "Cool." He kissed me again although there was less aggression and more hunger this time. "Sorry. I couldn't get away from the meeting. And I had no way of contacting you. I don't have your phone number. Am I forgiven?"

"After a kiss like that, I'd forgive anything."

He reached for my hand. "You know, I've been wanting this since I was about fourteen."

I made an excuse. "I'm a slow learner."

"You were dazzled by Jerry. Most people were. They never saw me. I was always in the background."

"Have you eaten?"

"Coffee and biscuits, that's all."

"Most places around here are closed now. Um, I'm not much of a cook but I'm an amazing culinary artist with the microwave. I can do you Indian, Italian, Thai, you name it."

"Italian is fine."

"Spinach and ricotta cannelloni or pumpkin and spinach lasagna. I have a freezer full."

"I'll leave it to you."

I was wide awake now. "You want some wine with it?"

"It wouldn't be Italian without wine."

I had a half bottle of Shiraz left over from a few days ago. I poured two generous glasses, taking a sip to ensure it was still all right. It was fine.

I placed his frozen dinner in the microwave before handing him his glass. "At least you don't have to worry about driving home."

"Why? Are you inviting me to stay over? What happened to dating first?"

I'd been sipping my wine and his comments took me by surprise because I'd only meant about driving.

Wine spurted out my nostrils and I choked attempting to explain my meaning.

Matty laughed but thumped me on the back after grabbing a tissue for my nose. "It's okay. I was joking."

Before things could get any more uncomfortable, the oven pinged and I went to plate his meal. "It's nothing special," I spluttered, still attempting to get my breath under control.

"It'll beat a diet of sweet biscuits any day."

"Why don't you eat properly?" I asked

"Too many meetings, too much to do. I'm essentially a one-man operation."

"Sit. Have your meal. Talk later."

He quirked an eyebrow at me. "Is that all you want to do later? Just talk?"

"Behave yourself."

"I always found that difficult around you."

I went into the kitchen for some cheese and crackers because drinking wine on an empty stomach made me light-headed. Matt helped me demolish them as well after he'd finished his lasagna. He also polished off his wine.

"Any chance of a coffee while we chat?"

"Yes, master," I replied sarcastically.

"Hm, I like the sound of that. You on your knees taking my cock in that sweet mouth of yours."

That did it! I was officially hard. Since he arrived I'd been unsuccessfully attempting to keep my dick in check, but now it went from half to full mast in seconds. I didn't dare stand up because it would be so obvious in my sweatpants.

"What about that coffee?" he asked when I remained seated.

"You'll just have to wait a moment until things settle down."

He laughed loudly. "Did I excite you with my dirty talk?" He pushed his naked foot against my crotch. "You really are a big boy. I don't understand why Jerry ever let you go."

"Because he's straight," I replied.

Matt waved it away as if it was of no consequence. "Is he? I wouldn't know. I haven't seen the family since I was seventeen." He saw my look of surprise. "You didn't know? I suppose you didn't, although I thought Jerry would have filled you in whenever he came to stay next door."

"He never came back after that…day on the beach. Until a few weeks ago. The house was rented out after the Fittons left. Jerry came back to celebrate the sale of the house. Made a hell of a racket. He and his girlfriend insulted me."

"He always was an asshole."

A thought suddenly occurred to me. "He doesn't know you bought the house, does he?"

"He hasn't a clue. Did it all through my accountant. Screwed him out of the real value. Got it for a song."

"Why? What happened to you?"

I was only semi-hard now so I got up to make the coffee while he explained.

"That day on the beach…"

"The day you kissed me?"

That made him smile. "I couldn't hold off any longer. My balls were purple for you. After Simon attacked you, he and Jerry dragged me away, back to my grandparents. They were worried about the police. I was worried they'd killed you. Grandpa Fitton threw a wobbly when they told him what had happened. Their version, of course. You know, Sam Dempsey the pervert attempting to seduce innocent young Matt Clifford. I told him it was all a lie but they preferred Jerry's version, that way they didn't have to cope with a 'pervert' grandson. They washed their hands of it once Jerry told them about Simon bashing you. They rang my parents and told them to come and take us away as fast as possible. I guess we were gone by the time they let you out of hospital."

"It wasn't that serious, Matt. I was a bit wobbly on my feet and I stayed in bed for a day or two feeling sorry for myself—"

"I thought you'd ring and let me know. When you didn't, that's when I realized you didn't care about me at all."

"But I did ring," I reiterated. "Just about every day for two weeks. I mainly spoke to your mother who told me you never wanted to speak to me again. I didn't believe her. Then I got your brother who threatened to call the police if I didn't stop phoning."

We both sat and stared at the table, in my case regretting what might have been. It was making us melancholy. I changed the subject. "How did you become so successful?"

"The family made my life a misery. Jerry convinced them it was all your fault but I kept contradicting him saying that I had kissed you, and it was all my fault. My dad didn't want to hear his son was gay so he warned me. 'I know you're just trying to protect your mate,' he said. 'But if I thought for a moment you were queer, I'd send you away for treatment. Not let you back in the house until you got such perverted ideas out of your head'."

"Shit," I sympathized.

"I heeded the warning. I shut my mouth. I knew my time was short so I began selling everything I owned. It wasn't much. Mainly music. My guitar. A few things I wouldn't need where I was going. Got a few part-time jobs after school. Played it cool. The oldies thought I was buckling down and being very responsible. Meanwhile, I put out feelers to the surf community. Learned where the money was in competitions. About nine months after I was dragged home, I packed everything I owned in a duffel bag, grabbed my board, took a few extra bucks from a jar mum had in the kitchen for a rainy day. It wasn't gonna get much rainier than it was for me. I got myself to a mate's place and he allowed me to sleep on his couch. He wasn't someone from school, so my parents had no idea where to look for me. That's if they even bothered – which I doubted."

"You sure were a brave little guy."

"Not that little. I was seventeen by then. I bummed around for a year or so, going from one championship to another, winning minor prize money until I realized I was never gonna be a big name. Occasionally, I'd get work in a board factory to make ends meet. I really got off on it. I thought that might be something I'd like to do. I needed to settle. I needed to get myself a skill or two. Then I'd come looking for you. I'd track you down. And here I am."

"Did you know I still lived here?"

"No. I was hoping, of course. But I bought the house next door because I spent some of the happiest days of my life there. The summers when I could see you."

I got a little choked up and a little teary. This hot man seated at the table opposite me was telling me he'd fancied me. He could snap his fingers and have any man he wanted. "You're not a virgin?"

"Hell, no. The mind is willing but the flesh is weak. I knew, too, I'd stand a better chance against all those hot guys who'd be throwing themselves at you if I had some experience. Don't get me wrong, I wasn't a slut. I only went with guys when thinking about you hurt too much."

"Oh, God, Matty."

I was out of my chair, wrapping my arms around him as he began to sob. "I always hoped you'd still want me. Want me the way that kiss told me you did. I never lost hope."

Lifting him out of his seat I took his hand and dragged him to the bedroom. I wasn't after sex, I just wanted to cuddle him, make him feel safe, make him feel wanted. We lay on the top of the doona, fully clothed, although I ached to feel his naked tanned skin against mine. He snuffled a few times into my neck, mumbling an apology, and then fell asleep. I couldn't remember the last time I had a man cling to me or even sleep in my bed. I liked it, especially as it was Matt. Sweet Matty. I must have dozed off as well.

It was the feel of a tongue rubbing against one of

my nipples that woke me. I was naked. How did that happen?

"Oh, good. I hoped you'd wake up. No sense in doing this if you weren't going to be awake enough to get any pleasure out of it."

"Any pleasure out of what?" I mumbled rubbing my eyes because the room was in darkness and I could barely see Matt's shadow. Under the circumstances, I didn't need to see anything because he suddenly wrapped his mouth around my all-too-solid prick and began to bob his head. It took more energy than I had merely to groan, even though he was doing all the work. I managed to lift my hand and place it in his beautiful blond locks, running the strands through my fingers. He bumped his head up, suggesting he liked what I was doing. I tugged less gently and he hummed his appreciation around my cock.

"That is so good, Matt."

He palmed my balls with his free hand, stroking his way down to my butt crack, probing my warm hole with his finger. My body almost arched off the bed when he slowly pushed his finger inside me. He choked a little on my cock as I inadvertently rammed it farther into his throat. He gasped for air momentarily before sliding his lips down my shaft again, flicking the head with his tongue.

I couldn't believe I was actually doing it with Matt. After all these years, it was as good as I'd fantasized in my moments of self-indulgence. It all stemmed back to that kiss. "I've wanted this for so long, Matt. I dreamed of this."

I didn't expect him to say anything, he merely increased the suction around my cock in what I believed was agreement. He was a sexual dynamo and there was no way I could extend the pleasure I was getting from his expert mouth. I was ready to blow my load. I tapped him on the shoulder to signify I was close, giving him the opportunity to take his mouth away. I would have loved to watch my spunk spurt all over his handsome face, marking him as mine. Maybe next time. If there was one. I sure hoped there would be.

He kept his mouth clamped firmly to my cock and the first spray disappeared down his throat. He must have wanted to taste me because he eased back until my cock was on his tongue. A few more bursts and I was done, my cock popping out of his mouth. I heard him swallow. "Sweet," he whispered before licking the residue from my knob and scampering up my body to plant a wet sloppy kiss on my lips.

"You got any lube?" he asked.

"Bedside table."

He clicked on the lamp and scrounged in the drawer for the grease. I expected him to switch off the light but he left it on. "I want to watch your face as I fuck you."

"What if I don't like being fucked?"

"Then you'd better learn to like it. I intend to do it to you on a regular basis."

I guess that answered the question about whether this was a one-night stand. "What if I want to fuck you?"

Matt grabbed hold of my stiffening cock. "That can be easily arranged. Any time you want."

"Well, that answers the two most important questions I had."

Matt lubed his fingers and slowly inserted two into my hole, stretching me for his cock which, until now, I had never seen. He was bigger than me, thicker but about the same length.

"Use plenty of lube," I begged.

He liberally greased me before he shucked my legs over his shoulder, lined his cock up with my entrance, and slowly entered. Normally, I would have been grinding my teeth at the burn but because it was Matty, I welcomed the slight pain. "Do it, Matt. Fuck me hard." He sank up to his balls, his cock entering my anus like a hot knife through butter. I was hard again. I wanted to feel him, feel him like I'd felt no other man before. He picked up the pace, ramming his prick in and out, hammering me into the mattress. He was concentrating on bringing me as much pleasure as he was getting. I could see it in his face. Too many men before him were so transparent it was written large in their eyes they didn't care about me as they fucked my ass, they just cared about dumping their load as pleasurably as possible.

"I knew you were worth the wait, Sam. Your ass was made just for my cock. You feel it, too, don't you?"

I did but he was doing such incredible things to my body all I could manage was "Uh huh."

"Come for me, Sam," he said jerking my cock with his still slick hand. I'd never come twice in such a short period of time but for Matt I would. As he found my little bud of pleasure, making me gasp every time he drove his prick over it, he increased the pressure on my cock until I could no longer hold back. I plunged my ass down on to him, my emotions raging as I squirted all over my belly and chest, Matt continuing to hammer me in an effort to catch up. Moments later, he made a series of grunting sounds, ramming home each spurt until his balls were empty. "Holy fuck," he whimpered.

I guess we should have got up to wash the spunk off our bodies but there was something so right about leaving it until the morning, the dry crust a reminder of what we'd been up to. He muttered, "I love you, Sam.

Always have. Always will." I kissed his nose and said "I love you, too, Matty" but he was already asleep.

I wondered if, perhaps it was too soon for the L-word but, hell, we'd waited ten years.

CHRISTMAS IN JULY

"Kauko Sallinen, you are an idiot." I didn't say it out loud, I merely thought it. I'm not really an idiot, although I'd be hard pressed to prove it by my behavior on this occasion. I'm in the top ten in my IT field, usually excellent at everything I do. I guess that also includes my newly discovered expertise – getting lost. Right now, I was wet, miserable, literally shaking with cold, and to cap it all I had no idea where I was. Did I mention I was injured?

Normally, I have a great sense of direction; can find my way out of anywhere, including multi-level underground car parks. Not so here on the other side of the world. It's not totally correct to say I had no idea where I was because my current location was somewhere in the Megalong Valley in the Blue Mountains, 115 kilometers west of Sydney. I assumed I was still in the Megalong Valley as I seemed to have walked an incredibly long time, so I could have been in China for all I knew. My internal compass was shot to pieces since I arrived in Australia from my native Finland.

So what was I doing on the geographical underside of the world in a country whose weather was the antithesis of my home? Long story. Almost as long as the flight to get here to escape the misery and heartache I'd left behind. I wanted out even though my family and friends told me I was making the biggest mistake of my young life. They understood the part of wanting to leave Vaasa on the west coast of Finland well enough – they knew I would have to do that eventually anyway to make the best use of my talents – but they assumed I'd head somewhere closer, such as Helsinki, maybe somewhere in Europe, at most the U.S., but Australia?

My choice of destination was greatly influenced by the offer of a job with an up-and-coming IT company that lacked someone with my skills, but also the positive feeling I got from the CEOs of the company, young guys like myself who were full of fire and love for technology, obviously on the brink of international success. I so wanted to be part of that rather than just another cog in a very big techno wheel in Silicon Valley. They offered opportunity for advancement, with an option of shares in the company, but the cherry on the ice cream was the fact their offices were in Sydney. Visions of warm, sandy beaches, hot summers, hotter men. I'd dreamed about that for most of the twenty-four years of my short life, beginning when I'd collected colored cards of Australian marsupials from breakfast cereal packets as a kid. In fact, the cards were still in an old cardboard box under my bed back home in Vaasa. My mum was convinced if she kept my room as it was when I left that I'd return. She was reckoning without Esa.

The reason I'd become lost had to do with those self-same collected cards. I'd been informed by Kylie, the helpful young woman at the front desk of the Hydro Royale, a faded old grand hotel and spa that had seen better days but which was now being slowly restored to its Victorian splendor, that the valley was full of the sorts of creatures that were depicted on those cereal box cards. I'd already cuddled koalas and given kicking kangaroos a wide berth, fed popcorn to an emu, and been bowled over by an aggressive wombat in a touristy animal sanctuary, but what I really wanted more than anything was to see these and other animals in the wild.

I realized now that Kylie had been exaggerating the wildlife numbers, probably in a well-meaning but foolish attempt to impress a visitor because, in my frustration, I'd wandered off the main track, as dilapidated as it was, in an effort to see the real Australian bush. Well, I was seeing it in abundance except that drizzle had begun to fall, the temperature had dropped precipitately, and mist was rolling in, making the conditions damp and slippery. The one consolation was that the bush was beautiful in these conditions. It also brought out a number of the creatures who relished the wet weather. I heard what I believed were lyre birds although I didn't glimpse them.

I heard twigs snap behind me and in turning to catch a glimpse of some untamed marsupial, I slipped, twisting my ankle in the process and landing face down in the mud. My camera survived the fall but I couldn't guarantee it would be in any sort of working order given the dirt and leaves that now covered it. Pushing myself up onto my knees, I thought of calling for help, but apart from a few hikers kitted out for a lengthier trek than I'd attempted, I'd seen few people on the trail. The most recent had been over an hour ago by my reckoning. Most people preferred the more comfortable boardwalks through the rainforest in nearby Katoomba.

I attempted to stand but there was no way my ankle would support me and I crashed to the ground, groaning in pain. I would need some sort of a crutch. There was nothing to hand so I crawled on my hands and knees a few meters along the track until I found a small fallen branch of a gum tree. It would do as a makeshift walking stick as long as I could trim the excess from it. My trusty Swiss Army Knife made short work of pruning the support before I hoisted myself aloft. It enabled me to stagger forward slowly so that at least I could search for shelter. The continuing spatter of rain on my damp hair and down my neck irritated me to such an extent I couldn't think straight.

It was quite a walk before I discovered anything even remotely approximating shelter. Normally the trees would have been enough but the rain caught in their leaves and dripped down on me like Chinese water torture. Up ahead, I discovered a large rock overhang. It wasn't a cave but it was a roof to protect me from the rain pellets, if not the cold and damp. I prodded the darker recesses in the search from anything lethal such as snakes, giant spiders, crocodiles, sharks, or hairy bunyips that supposedly disposed of millions of Aussies every year. Yeah, I'm exaggerating, but I still didn't fancy sharing my newly discovered refuge with scaly or hairy venomous critters.

Once I'd ascertained I was safe, I made myself comfortable on a flat rock, extracting my mobile phone from my muddy jeans. No luck; it was a zero signal zone. I ducked out from beneath the rock just in case, but my hopes were dashed. Still no signal.

What with the freezing conditions and the moisture that permeated my clothes and my hair, my thoughts turned pessimistic. Would hikers discover my body in a week, stripped of most of its flesh by predatory wombats… oh, wait, wombats are vegetarian…but you get my drift anyway. I couldn't rely on a search party being sent out to look for me. No, my best bet was to keep moving once the rain let up and try to find somewhere that my cell phone could pick up reception. I switched it off to conserve the battery. Good, I was thinking smart now.

But that's as far as it went. My clothes were wet through. I couldn't take them off to dry because they wouldn't in this weather. Perhaps when the rain stopped I'd be able to find some dry kindling or leaves to start a small fire to warm myself and dry my garments although the weather looked as if it had settled in for a long stay.

My only realistic hope was my first thought – to keep moving even though I had no idea whether I was moving toward or away from the hotel at the top of the cliff. The bush was too dense. I needed to head toward high ground which might then give me a view of the valley so I could pinpoint the direction of salvation. I knew I had to keep to the track and not take short cuts because if the hotel staff missed me, a search party would stay on the trail. I'd heard of helicopter rescues in the area as well but they wouldn't be out in the rain. I had a red scarf, so I'd make sure to keep it unfurled to make myself a bigger target for rescuers to spot.

For the moment, though, all I could do was try to keep as warm as possible and not to panic. Easier said than done. One thing I knew for certain, I would wait until the rain eased as it was now bucketing down, forcing me farther under the rocky outcrop that protected me. I shivered in the cold, wondering if, perhaps, hypothermia might claim me before the rain stopped. My teeth chattered like castanets as I lay down in the dirt and curled myself up into a ball in an attempt to keep warm. I muttered a generic prayer, sending it out into the world, hoping that if there were a greater deity he, she or it might hear me. I didn't put much store in imaginary friends.

Someone or something must have heard my plea because I was awakened from a semi-conscious state by a shrill call of, "He's over here."

"Are you okay, son?" a kindly voice enquired. He felt my face and my hands. "You're freezing."

"I've hurt my ankle," I whimpered.

Turning back to the path he called, "Bring the blanket."

Another two saviors squeezed in under the overhang, water dripping from their wet weather coats and hats onto my body. I shuddered with the contact. "Let's get him out of those wet clothes."

My initial rescuer helped me to my feet, supporting me in his strong arms. I remained passive as the other two stripped me of my wet clothes and then began to massage my arms and legs to get the blood flowing. It felt good to be alive and I broke down, sobbing in relief.

"It's okay, mate. You're safe now," the guy holding me up said kindly.

They wrapped me in blankets, covering me in plastic to keep the rain off, before stretchering me out of the valley. It was hard going and a few times I thought I was about to be pitched into the undergrowth when one of the stretcher bearers lost his footing. They all chatted amiably, attempting to keep my spirits up, although it was totally unnecessary because I knew everything would be all right – as long as they didn't drop me. In fact, I felt so snug and secure, I lapsed in and out of sleep.

They told me later, it took two hours to get me back to the safety of the hotel where a concerned Kylie had raised the alarm when I hadn't returned once the rain set in. Three of the more experienced hotel staff had set out to find me as they assumed someone from the top end of the world would have little experience of the bush, especially in wet weather. Embarrassed by my incompetence, I attempted to make up for it with profuse thanks which got on people's nerves until Nick, the head rescuer, snapped, "Shut the fuck up with the thanks or we'll bloody well take you back and dump your sorry ass in the bush."

"Okay, I get it," I said sheepishly, wondering whether he'd get upset if I offered him a blow job as thanks. He was a real cutie. I was out of luck because, it seemed, Kylie was his squeeze.

Nick helped me up to my room even though I begged to be allowed to stay in the cozy bar/lounge area which was dominated by a roaring log fire. It hadn't been my favorite room at first because a large Christmas tree adorned with tinsel and colored balls, as well as angels and reindeer, and small red Santas, filled a corner. It was complemented by the never-ending soundtrack of carols being piped through the hotels PA system.

I knew I was on the other side of the world but did they really celebrate Christmas in a totally different month to the rest of the world?

Kylie laughed when I asked her the first day I arrived – was that just two days ago? – explaining that it was a tradition to celebrate Christmas at the hotel in the month of July for those who couldn't acclimatize to the heat and humidity of a Sydney summer Christmas.

It was a money-spinner for the establishment in what was otherwise a slow tourist period. I'd known none of that when I'd booked in. I'd been in the country just a few weeks and was giving myself a well-earned break before beginning in my new employment. I wondered how they'd feel when I hobbled in on crutches to start work.

Nick helped me onto my bed. I was guilty of clinging to him much more needily than was necessary because I'd had very little warm human contact since I'd flown out of Helsinki. A few quick fumbles had been enough to quench the itch but what I longed for was someone to hold. I hadn't had that sort of contact since…I didn't want to go there.

"You're in luck." Nick smiled as if to indicate he knew perfectly well what I was doing in holding on to him way too tight. "There's a doctor staying at the hotel and he's agreed to have a look at your ankle. We weren't too confident of getting anyone local to come out in this weather. There's even a report that we may get snow. Doesn't happen often but when it does we get a big influx of visitors from the city. Anyway, I'll send up a tray of sandwiches and tea? Coffee?"

"Coffee would be great." I was about to thank him again but he must have read it on my face and just put his index finger up to stop me. "Don't," he said. I grinned sheepishly and the gratitude died in my throat.

He left me then to luxuriate in the warmth of the room and to worry about my ankle. Sitting propped against the pillows of my bed I wanted to examine my injury but it was covered by a thermal sock the rescuers had put on my feet. By comparing the two, however, I could see the left ankle was swollen.

It was around noon back home so I decided now was a good opportunity to ring my parents before my supper arrived. Leaning across to the night table to grab my laptop, I settled it on a pillow on my thighs before opening it to use Skype. My dad would be at work but mum would be home. It had been a few days since we'd chatted and I knew she worried unduly. I was the first of the four siblings to leave home.

"Hi, mum," I said when she responded.

She shrieked happily like she always did as if it had been months between calls. Less happily she also insisted on filling me in on everything that had happened to family and friends. After she'd enquired about my health – I didn't tell her about my recent accident – and I'd explained where I was and we'd laughed about the peculiarity of people celebrating Christmas six months early, I let the comfortable familiarity of her voice lull me into a state of calm. She'd always been the one to soothe away the physical and emotional pain.

Like she did when Esa and I split up. I guess it wasn't so much a split as a tear when I gave him his marching orders. I thought I was living the dream. He moved into my apartment not long after we met and I fell in love. At least I thought I was in love even though he disappeared for long periods of time for his job – or so he said. He was a tablet designer for one of the generic Finnish brands and, as a result, he spent a lot of time out of the country. He always promised that one day he'd take me with him on one of his sojourns to the Big Apple and those foreign parts that were mere names to me.

I'd been devastated when I discovered that the time spent away from our home was with his wife and two children in Helsinki. There was no international travel, there was merely quiet domesticity within the confines of a conventional marriage. The only real thing about him was his first name. All the rest was fictitious, right down to his sworn explanation that his marriage was a sham and that he was currently working out ways to get out of it so he could be with me permanently, when I confronted him with his lies. Fools in love will believe any shit they're fed. Consider me well fertilized. I actually believed him.

It was months before it occurred to me that he'd lied again. I changed the locks on my door, donated all his clothes to charity, sent him an email telling him what I'd done, and then blocked his replies.

It was mum who held me while I cried my heart out over the fucker. She never said, 'I told you so' even though she'd never liked him. For starters, she thought he was too old for me. I thought he was perfect. He was mid-thirties, distinguished rather than hip, settled, attentive – everything a guy my age is not.

"You're not listening," my mum said over Skype.

"Sorry, my mind wandered. I'm tired."

We chatted for a while longer until I heard a knock. "Gotta go, mum. There's someone at the door."

"You look after yourself, you hear? And keep in touch so we know you're safe."

"I will. I promise. Love you." I disconnected. "Come in," I shouted.

The door opened and suddenly my whole world changed. The sexiest man in the entire world opened the door bringing in a tray of sandwiches and a pot of coffee.

"What happened to Nick?" I said rather rudely. I'm always flustered by good-looking men.

"They're really busy downstairs. He asked me to look in on you so I thought I'd bring your snack up as well to save him time." He came over to place the tray on the bedside table after he'd moved a few of my personal items aside. He glanced at the gay romance novel I'd been reading, making me blush to the roots of my hair because the cover was of a silver daddy, stripped to the waist to expose his very prominent abs and pecs, fighting some unseen enemy while protecting his equally gorgeous young lover under a finely muscled arm.

He tried not to smile as he asked, "Good book?"

I was too intimidated by his handsome appearance to snap back at him, so I settled for, "If you like that sort of thing."

I was hoping he'd say that he did. No luck.

"I'm Dr. Miles Mathieson," he said by way of introduction. "Nick said you'd hurt yourself and, under the circumstances, what with the weather much too threatening to call out a local GP, I told him I'd drop in and take a look if that's all right with you."

"That's fine. Did he tell you how it happened?"

He nodded. "You were lucky they found you when they did. The temperature has dropped considerably. How do you like your coffee?"

"I can do that," I said, irritated that he was treating me like an invalid. As opposed to what? A lover? I could only wish. I needed to slap myself about the face. My imagination was running off with me again. I needed a boyfriend and I doubted Dr. Kildare here was gonna be available to fill that gap. There was nothing to suggest he was even remotely gay.

"Lie back and enjoy being taken care of, young man," he smiled.

"I'm not that young." Shit, there went my mouth again. He might be into younger guys.

He laughed. "How old are you?"

"I'm almost twenty-five."

"Still a baby," he said.

I couldn't help myself. "How old are you granddad?"

That got a belly laugh from him. "Thirty-six."

If only I'd learned to shut up. "And how come when Australia changed over to the metric system they didn't make you change your name to Dr. Kilometers Mathieson?"

It was a stupid joke that he'd obviously heard before because he merely groaned. "This coffee pot is getting heavy."

"White, no sugar," I said wishing we could start this conversation over.

He poured the coffee, then watched me carefully as I sipped a little before placing the mug back on the tray. "Which foot is it?"

"The left."

Peeling the thermal sock down, he sucked in his breath as he examined the injury. "Nasty." After he'd prodded and squeezed while asking if it hurt – of course it bloody hurt, you moron – he gave me his considered advice. "Nothing seems to be broken but it wouldn't hurt to have it X-rayed to be sure. It can wait until the weather clears and I'll drive you to the nearest hospital or the doctor of your choice. Meanwhile, the best treatment is rest. And staying off your foot. Nick thinks the hotel has a wheelchair tucked away somewhere and he'll bring it up to you if and when he finds it. Don't want you missing out on all the fun downstairs."

He gave me a few more instructions and left a sample strip of stronger-than-normal painkillers. "This should tide you over until you can get professional help."

"What are you then? An amateur? You only do healing in your spare time?" Why do attractive men always bring out the bitch in me?

Fortunately, he took my sarcasm as a joke. "I'm on holidays. I don't get much time to myself so every moment is precious."

"Let me pay you for your time, doctor." I went to grab my wallet and fell ass-over-tit out of bed in the process, jarring my foot even worse. The string of profanities that issued from my mouth was enough to scorch the carpet. The doc rushed over to ensure I was all right. "Of course, I'm not okay," I yelled. "I just fell out of the fuckin' bed."

He laughed. "Why the hell would you do something as stupid as that when I told you to take it easy?"

"Probably trying to impress you."

He lifted me up as if I was a featherweight and placed me gently back on the bed. Not that I'm obese or anything like that but I'm still quite a bundle. All I wanted was to snuggle against his chest.

He seemed genuinely curious. "Why would you want to impress me?"

I snorted. "I guess my reading material outed me. So it won't come as a total surprise to you that I think you're hot."

"Hot?"

"Sex on legs."

"Oh." He seemed only mildly embarrassed by my flirtatious behavior. "There'll be no sweet loving for you for a while, young man. Your foot needs time to heal."

"I don't do it with my foot." I was so brazen, I don't know what had got into me.

He shot me down in flames. "It would be very unprofessional of me to become involved with a patient."

"But I'm not your patient. You said you were on holidays."

"You're a very persistent young man."

"You're a very attractive older man. It's a marriage made in romance novels."

He laughed as he moved toward the door. "It's been a most unusual experience meeting you Kauko Sallinen. I'll look in on you later this evening to see how you're getting on."

"Bring condoms and lube," I called.

Shit! Shit! Shit! I didn't even know if the doc was gay and here I was coming on to him like some sex-starved slut twink who propositioned everyone on first meeting. See what incredible looks do to me. That and the fact he was strong as fuck the way he lifted me back onto the bed. I'd felt the biceps straining under his button-down shirt. The doc was everything I look for in a man. He was breathing.

I was so embarrassed by my outrageous behavior I didn't think I'd be able to face him later. It was so unlike me but Dr. Mathieson pressed all the right buttons. Was he gay? Did he have a boyfriend? Did he like younger men? What were his kisses like? Damn. Now I had an erection.

Boring doesn't even begin to describe the next few hours. The programs on TV were a mess of reality shows, American cop dramas, and sitcoms. I couldn't concentrate long enough to get involved. I picked up my romance novel. There's something intensely satisfying reading all that man-on-man angst knowing that it will all turn out happy in the end. I didn't have the patience to expend all my energy on tragedy and pessimism. I was an old soul in a young body. That's what Esa kept telling me when I refused to watch the nightly news to which he was addicted. The world was a depressing enough place as it was, I didn't need to see the visuals of the world going to hell in a hand basket as well.

It's not like I was ignorant of world events, I simply refused to get involved. My heart went out to the victims of war and other tragedies, but I had a limited amount of compassion and I saved it for immediate family and friends. Esa called me selfish and self-absorbed among the many hurtful negatives he used to describe me. I preferred to think of it as self-preservation. Maybe I cared too much.

I went back to *Jimmy Starlight and the Barbary Pirate King*. It was pure fantasy of course, but then so is *Star Wars*, and no one seems to criticize that. As I got swept up in the adventures of the unrequited lust between the pirate king and the kidnapped English nobleman, I began picturing myself as Jimmy Starlight and Miles, Dr. Mathieson, as the wet-dream-on-legs pirate captain. I was still in the thrall of the adventure when there was a soft knock at the door. It was Jimmy Starlight who called 'Enter' and it was Captain Rackbeard standing at the door.

"Still awake?"

"Aye, captain."

"I said I'd pop in and see how you're going."

"Come in."

He sat on the end of the bed and untangled my foot from the blankets. His fingers scalded my skin where he touched me, my body so on fire for him, my cock already hard, as he scrolled off the bandage. I hoped he'd tug down my constricting clothing as well. Instead, he pressed against the swollen ankle, but I refused to cry out in pain. It wouldn't do to let him see I was afraid. I would endure anything to have him mine even if just for the night.

"It's healing nicely although I still recommend an X-ray," he said as he repositioned the bandage. "You'll be able to go downstairs in a day or two. As long as you're careful. Any other twinges?"

I felt like pointing to my crotch but that was pretty obvious from the tent in the blankets. I went for more subtlety. "Where I smacked my head on the ground when I fell. I have a bit of a headache. It might be concussion."

"Show me where it hurts," he said, moving to sit beside me.

I pointed to my brow and as he leaned in to examine me more closely, I grabbed the front of his jumper, pulling him toward me, to clamp my lips over his surprised mouth and dart my tongue inside. He struggled, but I quickly put my hands around his neck to hold him tight, concentrating on arousing his interest, if not another part of his anatomy. Exploring his warm mouth with my tongue emboldened me, especially when he stopped struggling and reciprocated, albeit tentatively. Careful to push my foot out of harm's way, I pulled him down on top of me.

I'd never been so brazen before in my life and I felt amazingly invigorated, like my blood was coursing with liquid Viagra, my cock grinding against his body as he scrambled to get more of my kisses. There was no reluctance on his part anymore and he seemed positively eager to get his hands on me. I almost backtracked on my behavior it was so alien to me, but if the action was at odds with my personality the feelings certainly were not.

It had been a long time since I'd been so turned on by a man. Whether it was a result of the aphrodisiacal qualities of my reading material, the lack of affection in my otherwise satisfactory anonymous sexual fumbles, or a psychological revenge on Esa, it didn't matter. I wanted Dr. Miles Mathieson in the best way possible – inside my body.

He broke contact to breathe. Looking me in the eye. "This is so unprofessional. But it's been so long."

I tried to assuage his guilt as best I could. "You're not my doctor. Why has it been so long?"

"Lack of opportunity. Don't be so personal. Besides, why don't you have a boyfriend?"

"Long story. Why don't you?"

"Mine's as long as *War and Peace* and has a lot of similarities apart from length."

I smiled. "Are we talking length of stories or length of…?" I reached down to squeeze his erection through his trousers.

Me and my big mouth; it broke the mood. The doc pulled away. "Look, you're a good-looking boy, you don't need an old guy like me making a pass at you."

"Old guy? You're exactly the age I like my men. And before you go on about daddy issues, you aren't old enough to be my daddy unless you got married when you were ten. Besides, you didn't make a pass at me, I seduced you."

He smiled. "Not often I get hit on by an attractive young man."

"You think I'm attractive?"

"Come on now, stop fishing for compliments."

I pretended to pout. "Anyway, you must get hit on all the time because you're gorgeous. And I bet your body is just as hot." I attempted to unbutton his shirt but he grabbed my hand, holding it still against his chest. Yep, I was right. His muscles were toned. I squeezed. "I knew it," I said in triumph and he dropped my hand as if it were hot coals.

"Flattered as I am–"

"Wait," I interrupted. "You're not going to tell me you're not gay? I won't believe you. That kiss was so hot you could barbecue sausages."

"No, I won't lie. I'm gay–"

I flung my arms wide. "Then take me, I'm yours."

The corners of his eyes wrinkled in amusement. "I appreciate the invitation, I really do…"

"Uh oh. There's always a but."

"You're too young to be so cynical."

"Not too young to have had his heart broken." I grabbed for his hand, attempting to pull him back closer to me. "I need specialist care, doctor."

"Nice try, but I'm a general practitioner, not a sex surrogate." He stood up to leave.

"You were hard when we kissed."

"The way you kiss would make the angels hard. What chance did I have as a mere mortal?"

I grinned. "Did you just pay me a compliment?"

"I'm sure you're intelligent enough to work it out for yourself. Now, if you'll excuse me, I have things to do, Mr. Sallinen." He kissed me on the forehead, escaping before I could wrap my arms around him.

It had been quite a day and I was happy to sink back in my pillows and dream of my very own warrior prince, Dr. Miles Mathieson. I did like him, and it wasn't just my dick talking. He was very pleasant on the eye, his body (what I'd felt of it so far) was impressive, he was kind, had a great sense of fun about him – and he kissed like a dream. All I had to do was work out how to get my lips on more of those kisses.

The next morning, Kylie brought my breakfast up on a tray, and I was so ravenous I devoured it as if I hadn't eaten in a week. At least my appetite had not been injured although my foot was throbbing enough that I took two painkillers to alleviate the discomfort. The cold weather outside seemed to have settled in and I was grateful once again not to be lying cold and damp – or dead – in the valley below the hotel.

My room was warm and cheery but I was itching to get out of bed and at least head to the more gregarious spaces downstairs where Kylie told me people who were not heading out on further tourist adventures were playing cards, watching widescreen movies, or propping up the bar. Alone, in my own room, the other activities sounded like the ultimate in pleasurable social intercourse. It hadn't been twenty-four hours and already I was going stir crazy.

Kylie was under strict instructions not to let me move from my bed until the doctor had seen to me. If I disobeyed, I was in danger of prolonging my period of incapacitation. Once I'd finished breakfast, I placed the tray at the end of the bed out of reach of my feet, sighing as I opened my sole companion – my romance novel – immersing myself again in its adventures. I would have to ration my reading as it was the only material I'd brought with me and I'd left my eBook reader at home thinking I'd have absolutely no need for it on this short break.

Whether it was boredom or sexual frustration, my mind substituted the very fine Dr. Mathieson – Miles – as the hyper-masculine pirate king, and myself as Jimmy Starlight. Their passion seared every page of the novel, the words tumbling headlong toward its consummation. I felt their every kiss on my own lips, their physical desire in my own groin. I was tempted to stroke myself as I read but if I came, and there was every chance that merely touching myself would cause me to erupt, I would lose the momentum of the writing and so miss out on the fictional climax. Perhaps I could judge it so they both occurred simultaneously.

No such luck. As the characters and I galloped toward completion, there was a gentle knock at the door. Damn. I managed to compose myself although not fast enough that there was not an impatient second knock. I cleared my throat but my voice was still croaky. "Come in."

The doctor put his head around the door. "I hope I'm not disturbing you."

He was, but I wouldn't tell him so. "No, come in. I was just sitting up. It's a bit of an effort with my foot the way it is." I straightened out the bedclothes in an attempt to disguise my erection, the doctor not quick enough to disguise the fact he'd been looking at the tent in the blanket.

"How is the foot this morning? Mind if I take a look?"

I stuttered. "Uh…"

His smile was so warm I wanted to snuggle into it. "If you would prefer, I can come back after you've taken care of…" he nodded his head in the direction of my embarrassment. "It's nothing to be ashamed of. Most men wake up with…um…morning wood."

I didn't like to tell him I'd been awake for several hours already and this was far from being an early wake-up erection. In the end, I didn't need to because the evidence lay in the folds of the blanket, the novel opened at the page I had just been reading. He picked it up. "Obviously this book stimulates your imagination." He glanced at a few paragraphs. "Hm, I can see why. I may need to confiscate this so you don't become over-stimulated." He was joking of course.

I think.

After examining my foot, his handsome face a study in concern, he took out his mobile phone to make a call. "Dr. Miles Mathieson here. I'm staying at the Hydro Royale and a young man slipped and sprained his ankle. I'm just a bit concerned it may be more serious than just a sprain. I was wondering if I can bring him in for an X-ray as soon as possible?...Yes," he looked at his watch. "That's quite suitable…" he spelt out his name. "One-thirty it is. Thanks."

Lying back in the pillows, I clutched the sheet theatrically, sobbing, "Will I…will I lose my foot, doctor? Will I ever be able to tap dance again?"

He laughed at my behavior. "Yes, I'm sure you'll be able to tap dance again."

"Wow, that's great," I replied. "I've never been able to before."

He shook his head as if he had no idea what to do with me. "I'm going to suggest you remain in bed this morning. I'll come and get you so we can drive to the clinic and get your foot X-rayed. I want to be sure there's nothing untoward. Just a precaution. Is that all right with you?"

"You're the doctor."

"Don't you forget it." He strode toward the door. "I'll see around twelve-thirty. Be ready."

"Oh, doc." He turned. "I'd like my book back, please. Unless, of course, you intend reading it to get a few hints on how to treat me even better."

He blushed and returned my novel. "I don't think you should be reading books like this."

"Why ever not?"

"It gives you too many ideas."

"I have enough ideas of my own as far as you're concerned."

He coughed to cover his embarrassment and fled the room.

What the hell was the matter with me? Flirtation is one thing, but I'd taken it to a whole new level – harassment. I needed to calm down. I desperately needed to take myself in hand. Perhaps my pirate fantasy romance was not such a good idea if I was going to be in a car in close proximity to Miles later in the day. I needed a good dose of reality. The cold shower that is morning television supplied enough mind-numbing banality and boredom that it also numbed my groin until I not only couldn't have managed a hard-on had someone held a gun to my head and demanded it, it also depleted me of the will to live. I barely had the strength to silence the inane chatter.

The remainder of the time before my appointment was filled with emails to friends and family back home. There was a message from Esa but I deleted it unopened. There was nothing he could say that would interest me now. He'd cheated on both me and his wife. That was unconscionable in my book. His feeble excuse later after he'd been discovered in his treachery was that his marriage was a farce, that he was going to ask his wife for a divorce, that they no longer had sexual relations but they'd remained married for the sake of the children. He trotted out every cliché in the adulterer's handbook, not even injecting an original thought of his own.

I wanted to believe him – who doesn't in my situation? – because I thought I loved him. But when I discovered he and his wife had no children, the whole lying edifice cracked wide open. Not only that, I discovered his wife was four months pregnant which meant she'd miraculously conceived by sitting on a wet toilet seat, she was as unfaithful as her husband, or Esa had lied about their lack of marital relations. Guess which one I chose to believe?

He broke down and 'confessed' that his wife had forced him into it. At that stage, I'd heard more than enough of his bullshit. I pushed him out the door of my apartment with instructions never to contact me again. His attempts at reconciliation fell on deaf ears and I deleted his voicemail messages without listening to them, his emails without reading them, and his personal intervention on my way to and from the shops and my place of employment with the threat of an apprehended violence order. In the end, I'd fled the country. And what did that get me? A sprained ankle. And an unrequited crush on a hot medico who was lifting me into a borrowed wheelchair in order to take me to the clinic in nearby Katoomba.

His body was warm and strong and I wanted nothing better than to run my hands across his chest and his muscular arms. Up close, Miles smelled of man musk and the slight aroma of his citrus deodorant.

As he carried me along the corridor because he'd been unable to bring the chair upstairs as the lift had been shut down because of a periodic service call, passing other startled guests who were out and about, my smart mouth had to comment, "Why, doctor, as much as I appreciate your brute force, isn't it usual to marry a guy first before you carry him off to ravage him?"

He stumbled, almost dropping me, before regaining his balance. "You really have to stop reading those books of yours, they give you ideas."

"Since when are ideas bad? Why some of the world's greatest discoveries came from ideas. Penicillin. Heart transplants. Electric razors. Shopping trolleys."

"They're not the sorts of ideas I had in mind."

I slapped him on the chest, taking an opportunity to feel his muscular pecs. "Why, Miles, what a dirty mind you must have." I was all innocence.

"If that's so, you put the thoughts there."

The doctor had dirty thoughts about me?

There was no opportunity to query him further on his rather suggestive statement as we'd reached the hotel foyer where Kylie waited with a rather dilapidated old wheelchair. "It's not much," she apologized, "but it should do for your needs, Dr. Mathieson." I didn't like the way she batted her eyes at him. I wanted to superglue her lids together; didn't she know the doctor was mine? He as good as admitted it a few minutes ago on the stairs. Or was I imagining it?

"Thanks, Kylie. It will do nicely,' Dr. Will-flirt-with-anyone said, his voice the consistency of warm honey. What was it with this guy? Did he turn his bedside manner on for everyone? *Hey, over here, I'm the one with the shattered foot that will require years and years of intensive up-close-and-personal therapy.* Miles, blissfully unaware of my internal thoughts, deposited me carefully on the seat and wrapped my legs in a tartan rug. With a final smile at Kylie, he pushed me toward the hotel entrance and the adjacent car park.

I remained silent and somewhat surly as he maneuvered me across the asphalt to his car. I knew if

I said anything, I'd sound bitter and sarcastic. I didn't want to come across as a total asshole, after all Miles was going out of his way to be helpful. I needed to appreciate that.

"You're very quiet," he said as he opened the passenger door before lifting me from the chair onto the seat, strapping me in tightly. "Is your foot troubling you?"

It was an easy out. "A little." I was such a fraud as I'd said it with just enough sincerity it sounded as if I was suppressing the true level of my discomfort. In fact, there was little pain at all.

He folded the wheelchair and stowed it in the boot of the car before climbing into the driver's seat for the journey along the Great Western Highway to Katoomba. It took around ten minutes as the traffic was light, although it took twice that to find the clinic and somewhere to park. Now that I was alone and in such close proximity to the hot doc, I was too shy to flirt and, as I had no small talk, there were a few moments of uncomfortable silence before he asked, "So, what's your story? What's a Finn doing so far away from home?" I'm not sure what it was – loneliness, lack of people to socialize with, a sympathetic ear – but the floodgates opened. Not immediately because I talked about my new job, but slowly, through astute questioning and a warm personality which belied the fact he was prying, I opened up to Miles. Besides, the chances of running into him again after I went back to the city were remote.

Eventually, I confided in him about Esa. It may have made me sound like a moral prig but Miles said, "Good for you sticking to your guns like that. Not often you hear a young man, or woman for that matter, stick to their principles, although Australia is a long way to run. Not exactly the center of world events."

I hoped he hadn't got the wrong idea. "With IT you can be just about anywhere these days. It's the new frontier, but my job isn't everything. I don't want to have a heart attack by the time I'm forty. Sure, I want a good-paying job – who doesn't? – but I also don't want to have to bleed for it. I want a career that interests me and pushes my boundaries. I suppose I sound like a cliché."

"Not at all. You want a life as well as a career," Miles said.

"Exactly."

"What about your…um…love life?"

"No love life at present. I experimented when I first arrived but the novelty soon wore off. I think it was mainly to see if Esa had crippled me emotionally. I really did care for him, you see. It still hurts sometimes. I needed to test the waters."

"Is that why you acted like a promiscuous trollop when you met me?"

My face went red. "It was a combination of the book I was reading and my feeble attempts at flirting. I'm not much good at reading signals. Besides, we're both on holiday and it's unlikely to lead to a long-term relationship. That, and the fact you're a very desirable man."

"You think so?"

"Uh huh."

"Thanks for the compliment. It's great for the ego."

"Tell me about you…"

"Here we are," he said, turning into a parking space just after another car pulled away. He scrambled out of the vehicle as if I'd asked to see his dick or something equally as inflammatory. The doc was running scared.

He retrieved the wheelchair and set it up in order to transport me into the clinic. I opened my door in an attempt to be less reliant on the kindness of strange doctors. Miles would have none of it, picking me up effortlessly and depositing me in the chair. It was cold out in the open and he wheeled me inside quickly, stamping his shoes against the damp seeping up through the asphalt. The clinic was crowded, mainly with people hacking and coughing, their noses blocked and red. Miles parked me well away from the colds and flu while he went to check at the front counter. The wait was short and in no time at all, my foot had been examined. We had an hour or so to kill before we could pick up the X-rays and the doctor's report so Miles asked, "Do you like hot chocolate?"

"Love it. Especially in this weather."

"How about we get out of here and I take you to one of the best places in the mountains for hot chocolate and cake? There are hand-made confectionaries as well. I have to pick some up as a gift for the Christmas party on the weekend."

"Lead on, Macduff."

He pushed me toward the main street of the town, drizzle threatening at any moment. "Why do you celebrate Christmas in July?" The idea puzzled me.

He laughed. "It's only a few hotels that bother. It's just a marketing strategy born of nostalgia for those cold Christmas holidays of the northern hemisphere. Just wait until you've had your first hot Christmas Downunder, you'll probably miss the snow of Finland. It won't seem like a real Christmas to you here."

"I'm not sure Christmas seems very real to me anyway."

We stopped in front of an Art Deco café named the Paragon and Miles went inside to ensure there was a table available. He re-emerged with a young waiter and between the two of them they hoisted me up and over the front steps and into the warm wooden interior, the walls lined with old-fashioned booths. Miles lifted me onto the seat and the waiter folded the chair, taking it away for safekeeping.

"This is wonderful," I said after I'd taken in the beautiful décor.

"Isn't it? I come here every time I'm in the area."

"They make their own chocolates?"

"The apparatus is all upstairs. They do tours from time to time. You should come back when your foot is better."

"How about you bring me?"

"Don't tempt me," he laughed.

"I wish I could."

"Could what?"

"Tempt you."

"What makes you think you don't?" He looked uncomfortable, so I had to assume he was unavailable. Oh well, better luck next time. "Are you in a relationship?"

Miles looked as if he would rather not answer the question, so I wasn't surprised when he responded with, "It's complicated."

Isn't it always?

I knew a 'mind your own business' rejection when I heard one. Miles changed the subject by asking, "What do your parents feel about you being so far away from home?" As we sipped luxurious creamy hot chocolate topped with marshmallows, accompanied by a slice each of rich carrot cake, Miles looked almost relaxed while the subject for discussion was me but he deflected any attempt on my part to delve deeper into his personal life. I suspected by the time we returned to the clinic he would know more about me than my parents, right down to my taste in men.

We'd just about exhausted my paltry young life experience when I saw an opportunity to finally get some dirt on the gorgeous Doc Miles. Obviously anticipating such a move, he looked at his watch. "I think it's time to get back and pick up the results, don't you?" Before I could answer he'd gone to the front counter to pay the bill and pick-up a number of boxes of pre-wrapped chocolates he'd ordered while we waited for our hot drinks. The waiter wrestled the old wheelchair to the side of the booth and Miles helped me slide into it before wheeling me down the two small steps to the pavement and then to the kerb.

The weather was definitely on the turn and a fine mist blanketed the town. I shivered as the damp threatened to soak into my bones. Miles noticed. "Let's get you back," he said.

It was but a short distance to the car park, and Miles settled me into the passenger's seat, turning the heat up while he went inside the clinic to get my results, grinning from ear-to-ear when he emerged about fifteen minutes later carrying a large gray envelope that obviously contained my X-rays. He climbed aboard and stowed the results on the back seat. Without saying a word, he drove away toward our hotel. My inquisitiveness got the better of me. "Are you keeping mum because the results show I'll never walk again and you're afraid to tell me? Or is this some sort of payback for flirting with you?"

"I've got some good news and some bad news."

"Give it to me straight, doc. I can take it."

"Do you?"

"What?"

"Take it?"

"Are you having second thoughts? I have to tell you that if you decided to put the hard word on me now that I can't flee from you because of my injured foot. I'd be at your mercy."

"And if your foot wasn't injured?"

"I'd run toward you as fast as my legs could carry me."

He chuckled. "You're so easy."

"Damn you. Stop teasing me. So tell me, what's the bad news?"

He put on his serious face this time. "As far as the examining doctor can tell, it doesn't look as if you will ever have a career in tap dancing."

"You bastard," I hissed, slapping him gently on the arm. "What's the good news? You're going to succumb to my charms and ravish me as soon as we get back to the hotel?"

"As I said. It's complicated."

"Way to bring a guy down."

"You'll be pleased to know the good news is that your foot is just sprained. But you have to take it easy, let it rest for a few days before you go back to partying. Living your life as if nothing mattered beyond your next sex partner."

"Is that what you think I do?"

"That's not a moral judgment, Kauko. Isn't that what all young gay men your age do?"

"No, it's not, Dr. Mathieson. Especially not me. I never thought you'd be a closed-minded old fart."

The remainder of the journey back to the Hydro Royale I sulked while Miles had the sort of pursed lips that suggested he'd just sucked a lemon. A couple of times he appeared as if he wanted to say something to break the tension, but then obviously thought better of it.

Once we'd reached our destination and Dr. Mathieson had unfolded my wheelchair and helped me into it, I took off while he closed the door and locked it. It was hard going through the loose gravel, but by the time he caught up I was half way across the car park to the entrance to the hotel. I heard him sigh as he grabbed the chair's propulsion back from me. "If you don't mind, I prefer to do this on my own," I snipped.

His sigh was deeper this time and seemed to be tinged with regret but fortunately he didn't take me at my word and kept pushing the chair until we reached the warmth inside. I was grateful because my hands were aching and I thought I detected blisters but I wasn't about to let him know that. Once inside the door, I wrested control back and took off through the foyer to the safety of the entertainment room where I hoped I might get a little peace and quiet. It wasn't to be. A young boy was watching a cartoon on the wide screen TV while others sat around chatting or reading newspapers. A few younger guests were texting on their phones or tablets. The hotel boasted free Wi-Fi.

I regretted I hadn't brought my book with me as all the reading material had been taken and there was little else to do but mingle or watch the bloody antics of animated animals, and a snowman with a carrot for a nose. I wasn't in the mood to socialize and…wait a minute… the kid was watching my favorite animated movie.

"Is this *Frozen*?" I asked.

The kid didn't take his eyes off the screen. "It's my favorite," he said.

"Mine, too."

He looked at me then to see what strange adult liked a kid's movie or maybe to see if I was putting down his taste. Satisfied, he turned back to the screen engrossed. I, too, began to loosen the bonds of stress, getting sucked into the action on screen so that when the pivotal moment arrived, I spoke the lines right along with the character.

"Okay. Can I just say something crazy?"

The kid jumped in out loud with the next line. "I love crazy."

Then, before we knew it, he and I were carried away by the sheer exuberance of the music, singing along, not caring that we were so loud we must have been destroying everyone else's quiet. We belted out "Love is an Open Door" with such gusto that when the song finished we turned to each other with a smile of total satisfaction on our faces, and we high fived. The applause brought us back to reality. It seems most everyone had put aside their newspapers and tablets to watch and listen as we made total fools of ourselves. Strangely, I didn't care.

Neither it seems did the young boy. "That was cool," he said. "Wanna do it again?"

"Sure," I said. "But maybe a bit later. My name is Kauko." I held out my hand and he shook it.

"I'm Oliver," he said. "You've got a funny name."

"I'm from Finland. You know where that is?"

He appeared indignant. "Of course. I'm eight, I'm not stupid."

"You must be very intelligent then because I don't think most adults even know where it is."

"It's in the northern hemisphere squashed between Sweden, Norway and Russia. Its capital is Helsinki. Did you have a reindeer for a pet?"

"I wanted one but my parents wouldn't let me."

"Parents suck. I asked for a reindeer this year but I know I'll just get a boring old computer game as usual. Mum and dad have no imagination."

"You know who lives way up to the north of my country? Santa Claus." I sounded patronizing even to myself.

He rolled his eyes as if to say 'Oh, please, give me a break.' Instead, he said, "Santa Claus is as imaginary as the Tooth fairy. And God."

That took my breath away. "Whoa. You're a little young to be so cynical."

"I have every reason to be."

"Really?" I wondered what on earth would reduce an eight-year-old to such pessimism.

"You're not very observant are you?" He pointed to his bald head.

Oh god, I died a little inside.

"I thought it was the latest fashion."

"My mum wants me to wear a wig, but it itches. I've grown to like it the way it is now."

"Leukemia?" I asked quietly as if the word itself was contagious.

He nodded his head.

"You're very brave."

He reached over and gripped my hand. I noticed him bite his lips as if he was attempting to keep his emotions bottled up inside.

"I'm not really brave. I ran away from the hospital once when they were giving me chemotherapy. I hid under the stairs in the hospital and wouldn't come out until they promised to take me to McDonalds and buy me an ice cream. My mum doesn't like McDonald's. Or Pizza Hut. Or eggs in cages."

"Have you finished your chemo now?" I thought it was time to talk to him like a young adult rather than talk down to him the way most people do to anyone under puberty.

"Yes."

"And…" I got a little choked up and couldn't continue with the question.

"That's why we're here. We're celebrating Christmas early this year because I heard the doctor tell mummy that I may not make the one in December."

What can you say to something like that? I had to clear the lump out of my throat. "Are you scared of dying?"

"A little bit," he admitted.

"Do you talk to your parents about it?"

"I can't," he admitted. "They're not coping with it. You're the first person I ever told."

"It'll be our secret," I said. "And as long as I'm in the hotel, you can tell me anything, especially when you're afraid. Okay?"

"Okay. I just don't want mummy and daddy to be sad all the time."

An exasperated voice interrupted our conversation and I quickly wiped the moisture from the corners of my eyes. "There you are, I've been looking everywhere for you."

"I've been here all the time, mummy. I was watching *Frozen.*"

"I swear you'll wear that DVD out if you keep on playing it. And you don't want to bore all the guests. As well as this young man."

"Mummy, this is Kauko and he comes from Finland where the reindeers are."

She held her hand out. "Jane. You must call me Jane." We shook. "Now young man, time for your nap. You don't want to overdo it."

"Aw, mu-um. I want to talk some more to Kauko."

"I'm sure you'll have plenty of opportunities to talk to him while we're here," she said, turning an empty smile on me. She didn't seem to care one way or the other how long I was booked in for.

"It's okay," I said to calm him down because I could see he was getting agitated, "I'll be around until after the Christmas celebrations."

He hopped down off the lounge to grab his mother's hand. "Cool."

"Please don't use that awful expression. It gives me a headache," she complained. "As if I don't have enough problems as it is, your father is in one of his moods."

As they walked out of the room, Oliver turned to give a little wave. I waved back wondering how someone so young could be so much more mature than I was. I'd sprained my ankle, Oliver had a death sentence dangling over his head. It sure put life in perspective. I wanted to do something for the little guy to make his last Christmas memorable, But what?

Miles interrupted my contemplation. I looked at the clock on the wall; I'd been thinking furiously for over half an hour and I was still no closer to a solution. "You. Me. Upstairs. Serious talk," Miles said with determination.

I saluted facetiously. "Yes, mon capitain."

He shook his head as he pushed me toward the stairs. "Incorrigible," he muttered.

Once I was comfortable on my bed, Miles looked as if the last place he wanted to be was here with me. "Look, this is hard for me," he said, pacing back and forth at the end of the bed. "I shouldn't have said what I did. It was rude and I'm sorry. I hope you can forgive me."

"Yes, it was rude. You made assumptions based on your own prejudices. But why should you care? We're just guests in a hotel, you'll never see me once I check out."

"Damn it, Kauko, just shut up for a moment and let me finish."

Normally I'd be furious at an outburst like this but Miles looked so stricken that I didn't have the heart to berate him. "Go on. My lips are sealed."

"This is going to sound stupid. Here goes. I know I've just met you but you make me laugh. You make me feel things that I haven't felt in a long time. No, don't ask. It's personal. Maybe, if I get to know you better, I'll tell you. Yes, I'll definitely tell you. It's been so long since I've had close personal contact with another man…I think you're smart, you're funny, you're good-looking, and I had a really good time in the café today. I miss cuddling and kissing and all those other ordinary mundane things and…"

"Come here, Miles."

He came over to the bed like a beaten pup. I pushed the bedclothes aside. "Take your shoes, pants and your shirt off and hop into bed. No, don't panic. All you're gonna get is a cuddle and maybe a few of those delicious kisses. They're very moreish."

He attempted a smile but it was a pale imitation of the real thing. His professional demeanor had collapsed totally and my heart went out to him. What the hell had I done or said to reduce him to this wreck? I would do my best to heal him regardless.

Folding up his trousers and his shirt, he draped them over the armchair before pushing his shoes out of the way so he wouldn't trip over them if he needed to get up and go to the bathroom. He seemed nervous as he slid into the bed beside me and I cradled him in my arms, his head lying on my chest while I tried to mentally talk my cock down because it was very definitely interested in the hot man in bed with me and expected action at any moment.

"This is nice," Miles said, his breath tickling the sparse hairs on my chest.

"Mm," I agreed.

We chatted about the new IT position I was to take up in a little over a week, Miles's medical practice, about Finland and my first impressions of Sydney. We laughed. We touched. I found myself stroking his hair while he ran his hand across my chest, occasionally squeezing my nipples. I was enjoying the physical contact so much I really didn't notice Miles's hand was slowly moving lower until he ran a finger around my belly button before he hesitated at the waist band of my boxers. He seemed unsure whether to continue or whether I'd stop him. My cock had very definite ideas of its own and was lurking, stiff and ready, just inches from the elasticized band.

He paused for so long I knew I had to help the poor guy out. I put my hand on top of his to guide him lower until he wrapped his fingers around my cock. He began to stroke me leisurely. "Is this all right?" he asked.

"It's nice." It had been so long since I'd actually made love as opposed to a quick anonymous fumble in a steam-bath or some other venue dedicated to instant gratification. "Here, let me help you," I said, rolling my boxers down and off. "You should make yourself more comfortable too."

He soon followed suit and I got my first real touch of his cock. He was as hard as I was. I kissed him, dragging him on top of me because I didn't think my foot would support me if I tried to get off my back. Our lips and tongues fused together even though the pace was slow, albeit with such an underlying volcanic passion I was afraid my ejaculation was imminent. It had never been like this with Esa. He'd made love as if he had a train to catch even when he was spending the night.

Miles slid beneath the blankets, licking down my neck, across my nipples, deeper along my body until I felt his breath on the head of my cock. I groaned, pushing my hands to his head to guide him but he wouldn't be forced. He was going to take his time. He tongued my balls before licking his way along my shaft until he tickled the head with his lips. I thrashed about; pain shot through my foot as I arched my back the moment he took me into his mouth. I wasn't prepared for the small number of cock bobs before he'd taken me all the way down and I was lodged in his throat.

"Oh god, Miles."

He couldn't speak. He was too busy tending to my needs. We both tried to make it last but it was futile to fight against the sparks exploding in my brain from Miles's expert oral technique. I just hoped he'd love my reciprocation as much as I loved what he was doing. I exploded in his mouth and he swallowed me down, cleaning the last leaks with his tongue.

"Give me a few minutes to recover and I'll repay the debt."

I paid with interest.

We fell into a satisfied sleep and it was early evening when I awoke to discover I was alone. Disappointed, I wondered whether he was embarrassed by what we'd done, or merely wished to escape in case I asked for second helpings. I didn't have to wonder long because about fifteen minutes later he came back into my room with a tray piled high with two hot meals which he placed on the small hotel room table. Wrapping me in a blanket before carrying me over to our supper, he surprised me with the sort of kiss I associated with long-term lovers. He sat beside me and we ate in contented silence. I didn't want to spoil the mood by asking where we went from there and he seemed more preoccupied with eating than with making conversation. It was odd that neither of us felt the need to fill the long silences.

When we'd finished the meal and he'd piled the dishes back on the tray, he poured us both a richly aromatic coffee. "Am I missing anything downstairs?" I asked.

"Not unless you want to watch mindless television, play mindless card games, or stand around the upright piano for a singalong."

"How jolly," I said sarcastically.

"It's much more entertaining up here with you."

"I was hoping you'd say that. Wanna go back to bed and snuggle?"

"I thought you'd never ask."

He carried me back, ensuring I was comfortable before he joined me. This time I lay against his chest.

I didn't want to break the spell but I had to know. "Can you stay the night?"

His look of disappointment said it all. He was about to make some excuse but I closed his mouth with my finger. "I know, it's complicated. So let's just enjoy this holiday romance and not expect anything else of each other. Okay?"

He nodded.

We lay together watching an old black and white Bette Davis movie on the hotel TV in the room. It was *The Old Maid* also starring Miriam Hopkins and it was a real tearjerker. I felt wetness on my chest as Miles attempted to hide the fact that he was crying over the ancient melodrama. I pretended I didn't know what was going on.

He left about eleven o'clock but not before he assured me just before he closed the door behind him, "I'm not in a relationship, Kauko. I don't cheat either."

I was confused. I had no idea what he wanted. What he expected. I would just have to go with it from day-to-day. If it led anywhere, that would be great. If not, I'd have some wonderful memories of a week with a hot doctor.

The next day the lift was back in operation and I wheeled myself downstairs hoping I might run into Oliver again, if not Miles. Instead I got waylaid by a couple from interstate who wanted to discuss the parlous state of their garden. I had no idea what they were talking about but I nodded when it seemed appropriate, shaking my head and tsking at other times, and occasionally throwing in a word or two. They seemed well pleased by my reaction, promising they would seek me out the following day for further stimulating conversation.

I read a little of my romance novel, I watched a bit of television, I had brief conversations with other guests who wandered in and out of the entertainment room and the small bar. That's how I filled the next three days waiting for Miles to turn up for each evening meal with me in my room. Then we would go to bed. By the third day Miles was riding my cock as I lay on my back. The position didn't do much for me but while I was waiting for my ankle to mend there wasn't much else I could do. Besides, the look on Miles's face as my cock penetrated deep inside him was priceless and worth the modicum of discomfort. I just hoped I would get to take control before the end of the week.

We also found a comfortable position on our sides so that Miles could take a turn at my ass. I'm a great believer in reciprocation. So it was my feelings for Miles deepened even though a little voice told me not to get too deeply involved until I knew what 'complicated' really meant. I would have to ask him. It was time. That way I would know whether this was something serious or merely a holiday fling.

Oliver was watching television when I went downstairs the fourth day. He was as pleased to see me as I was to see him, not least because it saved me making conversation with other guests with whom I had absolutely nothing in common. At least with Oliver we shared a love of *Frozen*. It was two days until Christmas and I'd rung around to get a present for Oliver which I knew he'd love. I'd wracked my brain for ages until the obvious smacked me about the face. I'd spent almost an entire day ringing around to find it, but in the end, I had. It took every cent of my savings plus a loan from my parents but it didn't matter. My job paid well enough and I'd be back in the black in no time.

We sat quietly watching another of his cartoon favorites, *Aladdin*, and we both chuckled at the animated shenanigans of Robin Williams as the voice of the genie and I'd even attempted to cheer him up with a harmony on a couple of the songs but Oliver looked tired and defeated, dark circles under his eyes. I muted the sound on the film. "Is something the matter, Oliver? Do you want to talk about it?"

"Mummy and daddy are fighting all the time. It's all about me. I wish they'd stop."

I wanted to change the subject, to cheer him up if I could. "What have you been doing with yourself when you're not watching cartoons?"

"We went to the Jenolan Caves yesterday."

"Did you enjoy it?"

"I didn't want to leave. We only saw two caves and they were so cool. And I saw a platypus in the river." His enthusiasm was infectious and he was soon describing the sculptural stalagmites and stalactites and the animals they looked like and his melancholy lifted.

Later, as his enthusiasm waned, and he looked more exhausted than ever, he took my hand. "Do you believe in God, Kauko?"

Was he looking for reassurance? Some hope to cling to? I couldn't lie. "No, Oliver, I don't."

"Good," he said. "Mummy goes to church every day to pray for a miracle and she's angry with her god. I don't like it when mummy is angry or sad. It upsets daddy too."

"What do you think happens when we die, Oliver?"

"I think we get reincarnated."

That took my breath away. "You don't believe in heaven and hell?"

"Nah. That's all made up to scare people, so my daddy says."

"You believe you'll come back as an ant or a wolf or a wombat?"

"A vampire would be cool."

"You'd have to take real good care of your teeth."

He laughed. "No, not that sort of coming back. But our bodies are made up of all these atoms and so whether you get buried or cre…cremated our atoms are eaten by the bugs in our body or released into the atmosphere and are absorbed by the trees and the grass and the birds."

I hugged him, trying to keep the tears out of my eyes. "You're one really special little boy, you know that?"

"Not so hard, you're crumpling my shirt."

I released him. "I've got a favor to ask, but you've got to keep it secret, okay?"

"What sort of secret?"

"It's a surprise."

"Surprises are usually really disappointing."

"Not this one."

"I guess I can keep a secret."

"When you get up on Sunday morning –"

"You mean Christmas Day?"

"That's the one."

"It's not really Christmas. It's only make believe."

"I know. But when you get up that morning…do you usually get up early?"

"Way before mummy or daddy."

"Then I want you to come downstairs and I'll meet you right here and we'll go get your surprise. Agreed?"

He didn't look convinced.

"You've got to swear otherwise the surprise will be spoiled." I made up some elaborate oath and Oliver giggled as we administered it with lots of spitting and crossed fingers.

When we'd finished, he said in all seriousness, "I hope your surprise is better than mummy and daddy's. They're hopeless at surprises. They never listen to what I want. They always give me what they think I want. And it's usually rubbish." He looked about the room just for a second as if he didn't know where he was. "I think I'll go back to my room now." He hopped off the couch and wandered away looking for all the world like he was lost.

I checked the weather forecast for the rest of the week, crossing my fingers that for once the prediction would turn out to be correct.

My secret nightly tryst with Miles was becoming serious. My feelings were rapidly approaching the point of no return and I felt a certain amount of reciprocation on his part. If only he would loosen up and tell me about the so-called complications. After all, he wasn't a serial killer or a slave trader. Was he?

"Why won't you tell me?" I moaned that night after our explosive sexual calisthenics. I was tempted to split up with him solely on the grounds that I didn't think my health could stand another bout of screwing at that intensity. Miles had his hooks in me and I think mine had sunk into him well and truly. But still we had this barrier.

"I promise, Kauko, before you go back to the city and your new job. I promise."

"You know I'm developing feelings for you?"

"And you're one of the best things that's ever happened to me," he admitted.

"Only one?" I joked.

"I'm serious," he said. "I really will tell you. I just hope you'll understand. I love you, Kauko. I love you more than any other lover before you."

I kissed him hard.

My leg was healing nicely and I could hobble around the hotel now although I preferred the wheelchair just to be on the safe side.

Early Christmas morning (or Christmas in July morning) I was waiting downstairs next to the Christmas tree. I looked out the window onto the back lawn very pleased that the weather bureau had got it right. About half an hour later, Oliver appeared rubbing sleep from his eyes. He had dressed warm just like I'd told him to.

"Merry Christmas, Oliver."

He mumbled something incoherent.

"Come with me."

"Where are we going?"

"You'll see."

Kylie was already in and knew exactly what was going on because I'd had to clue her in.

"Hi, Olly. Merry Christmas."

Again with the mumbling.

"Close your eyes. Properly. No peeking." I opened the back door of the hotel, Kylie hovered expectantly. I had my hand over Oliver's eyes so he couldn't cheat. "You can open them now."

Oliver just stood there, his eyes getting wider and wider, his mouth dropping open. With one almighty shriek he rushed headlong outside into the blanket of snow that had fallen the previous night and was still falling. It wasn't all that thick on the ground but to a little boy who had never seen snow before it must have been magical.

"Kauko, come and see, it's just like in the cartoon. Just like *Frozen*. Can we build a snowman? Can we?"

"Sure."

It wasn't much of a snowman any more than the snow angels we created by flapping our legs and our arms on the ground were but Oliver didn't care. He threw snowballs at me and I pretended to fall down dead tossing smaller snow missiles at him underarm so they didn't hurt too much. We were making so much noise that other guests began to wander downstairs, a look of wonder on their faces as they saw the hotel grounds blanketed in white.

Oliver ran over to me, his face pink with cold, breathless with excitement. "Did you make it snow, Kauko?"

"No, Oliver. I don't have the power to do that."

"It's the best surprise ever."

"Let's go and see if we can find a sled in that big old shed over there, shall we?"

He was already running. "Yeah."

I caught up with him and took his hand. As we approached, the shed doors creaked open. We stopped to watch until they'd been flung wide. If Oliver had been gobsmacked with the snow I swear I could hear his little heart about to burst in his chest. He stood stock still scarcely believing his eyes. He turned to me. "Is this my surprise, Kauko?"

"Yes, Oliver. This is your surprise."

He held out his hands and I picked him up. He hugged me. "This is the best surprise ever."

"It's from your mummy and daddy and me."

He stared at me as if he expected my nose to grow longer.

I walked him over to the man who had opened the shed door. "Hi, Frank. Thanks for organizing all this with such short notice."

"It's a pleasure, mate." He held out his hand. "You must be Oliver. I'm Frank."

Oliver shook hands without once looking at Frank. He only had eyes for the two reindeer under Frank's control.

I'd pulled strings, paid money, called in favors from my family until we tracked down Frank and his animal park. Once I'd explained the situation he'd been only too pleased to get on board. His brother had died of leukemia when Frank was twelve. I was exhausted from all the plotting and scheming, grateful when Frank took Oliver from me to let him pet the animals. The cold was getting through to my ankle and I needed to go inside to warm up. I was half hobbling and half hopping when Oliver's mother appeared at the back door. I hadn't taken her into my confidence so I hoped she wasn't angry. Her eyes were glistening. She nodded to me as she went to join her son.

I turned back to watch them. Oliver was seated on the back of one of the reindeer, Frank holding him tightly. This was going to be a good Christmas. Then it all came crashing down.

Oliver called out in his loudest voice, "Daddy, daddy, come and see the reindeer."

I knew before I turned who was standing behind me. My heart shattered. I turned to face Miles. He looked stricken to have been discovered like this.

"You bastard," I spat, quietly enough that no one else could hear me. "It's complicated, you said. Yeah, fuckin' right, it's complicated. You're married. After I told you all about Esa, you turn out to be the same sort of bastard."

"I can explain," he said weakly.

"You had all the time in the world to explain, but you didn't. Goodbye, Dr. Mathieson."

"Kauko, it's not what you think."

I pushed past him, almost knocking him over in my haste to get to my room so he wouldn't see my tears. I barely kept myself in check as I asked Kylie to call me a cab to take me to the station at Katoomba, pleading a family emergency.

"Can't you stay for Christmas lunch at least?"

"Sorry, Kylie. Maybe next year."

I got myself upstairs and flung my clothes in my suitcase, taking one last look around the room. I went back downstairs and Kylie sent Nick up to bring down my bag as it was too heavy for me to manhandle with my foot in the condition it was. The taxi arrived within fifteen minutes and within the hour I was on the train back to the city.

My new job took my mind off Miles's betrayal and I flung myself into it so wholeheartedly I had no time for socializing. I still hurt. I still had feelings for the bloody doctor. Why didn't he just tell me he was married and I was his bit on the side?

It was about two weeks after the abortive Christmas in July. We were in August already, the coldest month of the year, and my dirty clothes had piled high with neglect. I sighed, the washing wasn't going to do itself. That's what my weekends had been reduced to. Cleaning up around my rented flat, licking my wounds, and jerking off to internet porn. I knew the hurt would subside eventually, but for now…

There was a faint knock at the door. It wouldn't be for me. The only visitors I ever got were Mormon missionaries and Seventh Day Adventists. I ignored it, but whoever it was knocked a second time and then a third, getting more insistent with each attempt. I flung the door open to abuse the caller, only to be confronted by Miles, tears streaming down his face. Before I had a chance to speak or slam the door in his face, he bawled,

"Oliver died this morning. I had no one else to turn to. I got your address from the hotel."

I dragged him inside, hugging him as tightly as I could, my tears streaming as freely as his own. We must have stood there for a good twenty minutes giving full rein to our emotions until Miles had no more tears left to shed. I walked him over to the lounge and sat him down. He was in a daze, seemingly incapable of comprehension. I made him a strong coffee and poured a good slug of brandy in as well. He pulled me down on the couch beside him.

"I didn't mean to hurt you, Kauko."

"Whether you meant it or not, you did."

"You know all Oliver talked about was you. When he couldn't find you to thank you he wrote you a letter." Miles extracted it from his pocket.

"What's it say?"

"We didn't read it. It's for you."

Opening it carefully, I unfolded the piece of notepaper inside. On it he'd drawn a snow angel like those we'd made on Christmas Day. He'd written Kauko over it. Miles glanced at it. "When he couldn't find you he thought you'd disappeared because you were an angel sent to give him his wish. He was convinced you made it snow for him, that's why he's drawn you as a snow angel. He told us he wants us to spread his ashes in the back garden of the hotel next time it snows, that way his atoms will mingle with the snow angels. Whatever that means. We promised him. Jane and I would love for you to be there."

"You should be with her at a time like this, Miles. I'll call you a cab to take you home."

"Jane's not at home, Kauko."

I suddenly felt sick. "Where is she?"

"We've not been a married couple for years except in name only for Oliver's sake. She has a boyfriend. I've had lovers. But we kept that side of our lives away from Olly. My boyfriends couldn't cope with sharing me with my son, especially when the demands of his illness intruded. They all walked away. That's why I didn't want to tell you. I thought you would too and I couldn't bear that. I didn't know you'd met Olly. If I'd known, I would have told you he was mine. I made a mistake, Kauko. The biggest mistake of my life not telling you so that I lost you. I'm sorry."

Miles was an emotional wreck and I couldn't stand to see him this way, especially as he had no one to lean on in his grieving.

"Come on, I'll put you to bed, Miles, and you can have a little sleep. We can discuss it when you wake up."

As he slept I thought over all we'd been through and I dredged deep to see if there was a sliver of love I still held in reserve for Miles. He'd lied to me but it was for altruistic reasons. He did say he loved me. We did get on really well together, although I'd have to learn to trust him again. He's great sex. My parents would love it if I married a doctor.

The more I thought about it, the more I smiled. I went into the bedroom to ensure Miles was sleeping peacefully. I kissed his forehead and then stood watching him for a while until his breathing slowed.

Yes, I could make this man happy. He already made me happy. Maybe something good would come out of all the pain. I unfolded Olly's angel and put it on the fridge door, holding it in place with a magnet from a local plumber.

One Year Later.

The snow was deep on the ground and it must have appeared incongruous to passersby that six adults lay flapping their arms and legs in an attempt to create the most perfect of snow angels. Jane and her boyfriend Paul, Kylie and Nick, Miles and I, our fun leavened by the seriousness of the situation, watched over by other guests and workers at the Hydro Royale, were concentrating on Oliver's last request. We'd all been affected by the death of the little battler and we were paying our respects, the occasion sad but I guess we were all pleased to be able to do this in his memory.

Even my mum was watching via Skype in far off Vaasa. Miles was now part of the family because I had taken him home to meet my parents and my siblings a month prior, on our annual leave together. I was just showing off the incredible man I'd decided would be my partner for life, relieved that he liked my family as much as they liked him. I was equally as pleased to run into Esa in the street one day so that I could introduce my new husband, rubbing his nose into the fact that I was now happily settled. I loved Miles even more when he grabbed Esa's hand to shake it in thanks.

"What for?" a startled Esa asked.

"If it hadn't been for you, asshole, Kauko would not have come to Australia where he has a high profile and equally high paying job. But most importantly, I never would have met the love of my life. So, thanks for everything."

I kissed Miles in appreciation. Esa had no comeback and merely walked away in a temper, almost tripping over a raised section of the pavement in his haste to escape.

"How's the divorce going?" I shouted after him. I can be a vicious queen sometimes.

I wrote earlier that I had taken Miles 'home,' but I realized, although I had family ties to Vaasa and to Finland, my new home was with Miles. It had been a struggle to begin with, Miles grieving for his son, me unable to trust him fully but, as the cliché would have it, time is a great healer. We now lived together in a modest apartment overlooking the harbor. It was purchased as a sign of his commitment to our relationship with a deposit from Miles's savings once he and Jane had amicably divorced. He and I were now the proud parents of a substantial mortgage, joined at the economic as well as the emotional hip, whether we liked it or not. Just as well then that we liked it – a lot.

Miles's friends took a little more convincing that I wasn't just after his money and a cozy ride for as long as I remained in the country, but, eventually, they realized I was playing for keeps. The only downside was that they rang me every time their computer played up. *Is it turned on?* Life was good.

But life could also be unbearably sad.

Our snow angels looked forlorn as we stood to say farewell to the remains of our little friend. We each took turns pouring a handful of his ashes onto our snow angels and then, "Love is an Open Door" echoed across the valley from the hotel's outside PA, and we sang with all the joy and gusto, tinged with the sting of regret and sadness, we could muster, about Love being an open door, saying goodbye to the pain of the past, and the fact life can be so much more 'with you.' I squeezed Miles's hand before he and Jane dispersed the remains of Oliver's ashes into the snow, the strong cold wind blowing them over the edge of the cliff, some of them rising higher and higher in the air before settling onto the trees and plants, the soil and the ferns, the creatures and the insects in the valley below.

THE GOOD, THE BAD,
AND THE CUDDLY

When you're the sheriff of a small lawless western town, you have to make it your aim to know everybody's business. If you don't then your life is as short as the fuse on a stick of dynamite and ends up the same way: fucked. Your body will lie moldering in the cemetery up on Boot Hill, food for the worms or else varmints that can dig their way down to your mess of rotting flesh.

Headstone was not entirely lawless but this far west of the capitol it was the law of the gun that prevailed rather than the law of them there political windbags who think they know what's good for us like we're rambunctious school kids who have to be shepherded into some sort of behavior as dictated by them. That way, they believed, led to harmonious co-existence.

There was nothing harmonious about Headstone. I'd been in the job for nigh on six years – a record for a local law enforcement officer. Most of my predecessors got sick of the hours, sick of the conditions, sick of the miserable pay, or else landed themselves in that plot of land on Boot Hill. Death is the ultimate destination for all of us but it came sooner rather than later to those who didn't make themselves aware of everything that went on in the town, especially the background of new folk.

Sure, a lot of itinerants were cowboys drifting west just looking for the next cattle drive, a few prospectors hoping to strike it rich on the goldfields of California, or a few dusty cowboys with a pocket full of pay and a mighty thirst for liquor, cards, and the girls on offer at Miss Kitty's, the cathouse above the Lazy Steer Saloon. Breaking up fights between cowboys with more liquor than brains in their heads was usually the worst I had to contend with. The solution was a night or two in the caboose to sober up. Occasionally, a young buck would let his gun do the talking and someone ended up dead – usually the green as grass young ranch hand who fancied himself as the next Billy the Kid, forgetting that The Kid died with a bullet in his back and that legends about gunfights on the dusty main street are just that: myths. Usually it was a bullet in the back from a blind alley or from an upstairs window, the culprit long gone before the sheriff was called. It was the way to settle an argument in Headstone, but not one that I encouraged, although I have a couple of deputies to clean up the mess.

I always met the stage that came through the town once a week on a Friday with the mail. Sometimes it brought a new whore to work at Miss Kitty's. The old ones moved on, or just got so damned worn out, or else married some poor rancher slob who thought he could tame her wild ways. It also brought a steady stream of preachers each of whom believed that talk of fire and brimstone was gonna bring his sort of god-fearin' soul redemption to the town. The best God men were those who understood their purpose was to tend their flock and leave the others be. Conversion wasn't part of God's plan for Headstone and any reverend gent who tried it was likely to end up in Boot Hill beside any sheriff who didn't learn to stick his nose in everyone else's business. A quick proviso to that for an officer of the law who wanted to stay alive was that anything he learnt in pursuit of his duty he kept to himself unless the circuit judge insisted it was relevant to the case.

We were deep in one of those hot dry spells when the ranchers pray for rain because the cattle are as parched as the cracked red earth, their bones so obvious under their hide there's little can be done but shoot 'em.

Puts both the poor thirsty steer and the penniless rancher out of their misery. I've seen too many men go under when the dry spell goes on and on like one of the Reverend Payne's sermons.

I was there at the coach stop the day he arrived. He was saddled with the right sort of face for a preacher of his ilk; the sort that proclaims that all life is sin and the more uncomfortable we are on God's earth then the more treasure we'll reap in God's heaven: the type of holy bullshit that appeals to them that barely scrape a living from the earth, while it gets up the nose of cowboys who know there's only the here and now and there ain't no treasures once the last sod is tossed in over their wooden coffin.

And on the subject of them there coffins; he brought one with him. The folk that greeted the stagecoach doffed their hats as it was unloaded from atop the coach. The reverend gentleman mumbled a few words which I didn't catch as the box was manhandled onto a wagon, along with his bags and a few small personal items. Jake, the coachman, saw me watching. He spat in the dust as he made his way over. "The holy man's wife," he said without my having to ask. "Died on the way to this godforsaken hole." He spat again in an attempt to dislodge the dust from his throat and lungs.

"Natural causes?"

"Nothing suspicious, Sheriff Haskell. So I was told."

"You met the lady?"

"Nah, she died aways before I took on the load, but it was passed down the line that she was a good deal older than the holy man and the journey was a chore for her. Not the healthiest. There's a certificate from the doctor who attended her and the sheriff in Thunder Bend. All correct. I saw to it myself before I'd let them load the poor woman on my coach. I know you like your paperwork, Sheriff."

"Thanks, Jake. Appreciated. Makes life a lot easier. Just pleased to know the right reverend gentleman is not planning on selling guns to the red skins."

"You're such a suspicious man, Sheriff."

"That I am. It helps me stay alive. Just the way I like it."

"It must be a lonely life without…someone to look after you."

I took Jake's meaning. I wasn't looking for a wife. My job was too uncertain and I wasn't about to risk someone else's affections by taking a bullet through my chest. Nah, best to keep my affections to myself. Not that I hadn't been tempted over the years. Life can get mighty lonely and a man needs companionship but the knack for courting is not something that's ingrained in a rough man like me. Doesn't stop the eligible widder women of Headstone from turning their attention my way, or mothers of unmarried daughters of a certain age inviting the bachelor sheriff to dinner. Hell, even some of Miss Kitty's litter have seen me as a way out of their horizontal business. None of them appealed.

They say I'd be a good catch. Reliable, brave without being foolish, I got prospects and when I look in the mirror at Miss Kitty's bathhouse after the barber has attacked my unruly bristles and tamed 'em as best he can, and my hair is trimmed so it don't flap over my eyes, I see a man that I'm comfortable with. A decent man, basically honest, loyal, and…let's backtrack here aways. I say basically honest cause there is one secret I carried close to my heart and very few that lived in Headstone knew about.

If you remember, Jake said I need 'someone' to look after me. That's the signal that he knew my secret. Most people would have said 'wife.' A wife is something I don't need. I've known since before God was a boy what my life would entail. I was young back then, happy to be one of those cowboys who lived a life herding cattle from one lonely place to another. The life was hard but had its compensations; wide open spaces being the best of them. I get jittery whenever I feel fenced in. I guess that's why I run a mile if anyone tries. Probably why I ran a mile when Colton, one of the other cow hands, got a little too territorial about what we did in the dark after the sun went down. A few years older than me and much more experienced in the alleyways of man love.

In many respects, I owe everything to Colton. He opened me up to new experiences. Yeah, you get my meaning, don't you? I was green. Sure, I'd used the cathouses along the trail but only so the other cowboys wouldn't be suspicious. The quick loveless fumbles with bored girls who made their living on their back showed me it was not only loveless, it was unsatisfying. I got more pleasure from stroking my dick at night while I was on watch. That's how Colton found me one night.

We'd struck up a friendship because we were the only men young enough to have been born this side of the Declaration of Independence. I josh, but the other men on the trail seemed so old. Now that I'm around the age they were I see young kids at the schoolhouse look at me with awe that I ever got to be so ancient. Colton was my teacher; he'd been on three or four major cattle drives whereas I was as green as the grass I'd once seen in a city park, trimmed and fenced so it looked too purty to be real. I'd reached down to touch it to make sure it was genuine because I had never seen anything so green. I must have seemed like that to Colton the night he caught me pleasuring myself in the dark and whispered, "Let me help you," before putting his rough hand around my hard-on, pumping it until I squirted all over his boots. I knocked him down for his sinful touching.

He kept away from me after that. I was glad because my face flamed whenever I thought of what he'd done. I could have stopped him; but I refused to accept my complicity. I'd heard about the perverts who rode the open plains looking for young men onto whom to force their bestial urges. The minister in our local church was full of fire and damnation about such practices. What those practices were I had no idea then. When Colton handled my manhood, those sermons came home to me and I reacted as I was taught.

I fell into fitful sleep most nights after that remembering the heat of Colton's hand on my dick until I ached to feel it again. I was one of the damned. Fighting the feelings made me surly and difficult to work with until the cook – a wise old Chinese guy who'd won and lost a fortune on the goldfields but loved the open spaces as much as I did – took me aside and told me that if I didn't mend my ways I'd be left at the next township we passed.

"I don't think I can," I admitted.

Yan lit his pipe and drew the smoke into his lungs. Whatever he smoked it smelled like burning rat's fur to me so when he offered me a chance to inhale the stink I turned him down – politely. He looked at me for a few moments, and then said, "I notice you and Colton don't bunk together anymore."

It was natural someone would notice, but it still surprised me. I kept my mouth shut because I didn't want to make trouble for Colton regardless of the heinous sin he'd committed on my dick. I'd heard about men like him who were nailed naked to trees along the trail and left to the coyotes and wolves. I wouldn't wish that on any man.

"He touched you?" Yan asked quietly. My face, crimson with embarrassment, gave me away. "Ah," he said. "So, that's it."

I nodded, lowering my head in shame. Instead of the condemnation I expected, Yan laughed. "You hit him, I expect."

Again, I nodded.

"Much like my first time," Yan said.

My head jerked up at Yan's admission. "You've—"

"I doubt there's a man on this cattle drive who hasn't done it with someone like Colton. They keep it to themselves. Sometimes, a man will be so…what's the word?…like the women who work in saloons that the men will share him, treat him like they treat those women. But they will forget him the moment they reach the next town that has a cathouse with girls. It's a lonely life on the trail. Men grab pleasure where they can. As long as they keep it out of sight, who cares what they do?"

"But, it's wrong."

Yan shrugged. "I know nothing about wrong. All I know is it brings pleasure and relief."

I was more confused than ever when I went back to my duties. It was as if Yan was giving his okay to what had occurred between me and Colton on my lonely night watch. As I couldn't get the feelings out of my soul, and I knew Colton had given me more pleasure with his one simple act than any of the trail-soiled girls I'd visited, I wondered if there was a lot more about the unmentioned life on the trail I could learn from him.

My conscience wrestled me into submission for over a week after Yan and I had talked, until I discarded it as old-fashioned and inappropriate for the current situation. Self-serving, I know, but deep inside I knew I wanted to experience that forbidden pleasure again. I waited until I knew Colton was on watch to make my play. It was a gamble. He could reject my advances, sock me on the jaw like I did him, or even tell the boss what I was up to. It didn't matter to me because my head was so full of what I now admitted to myself: I was one of those animals that lusted after his own kind. Colton's simple touch had awakened desires I'd managed to damp down: the longing looks I gave men when they bathed in the muddy creeks we traversed on the drive, the surreptitious peeks I gave their flaccid pricks as they pissed against a tree; the hardness in my crotch as I watched a cowboy's ass as he swaggered in front of me. I was damned because I knew deep down that I not only wanted Colton to touch my privates but that I wanted to touch his in the same way. I was doubly damned.

I suppose I could have been more subtle but my need outweighed my caution. Even so, nothing could have prepared me for Colton's reaction. I waited until I heard the deep snoring of men used to hard physical exertion before I cast aside my blanket and crept silently past the campfire to the outpost where I knew Colton was keeping guard, taking puffs from the cigarette that was stuck to his bottom lip in between snatches of the tune he was humming quietly to keep himself awake.

"Don't lurk in the shadows, boy," he said without turning to face me. "I can smell you from here."

That surprised me but, as I learned later, each man has his own distinctive odor for good or for bad. I'd just never been up close enough before to notice.

"You come to take another poke at me, boy? Cause if you have, I'll tell you now, the first one you get for free, try it again and I'll whup your ass but good. Then, maybe, if you beg nice enough, I may stick my cock inside you to give you more pleasure than you ever knew possible."

Did men do that to each other? I was so confused, I stuttered when I asked the question out loud.

"That and more," he replied, peeling the soggy cigarette from his lip and grinding it underfoot. He finally looked at me. "You here to learn or to damn me to hell? Because if it's to damn to me hell, boy, I've heard it all before and I pay it no mind. There is no hell 'ceptin' what we make here for ourselves on earth. Same goes for heaven. And it sure would be my idea of heaven if I could get me another touch of that fine thick cock of yours."

I was hard in an instant. Forcing myself to move forward, my feet lurching as if I was headed to my own execution, I knew in my heart I wanted to learn more and there would be no better teacher than Colton. That night we pumped each other's hard pricks enough to undo my mind, until near the climax, Colton reached for my head and pulled me in for one of those deep kisses that only whores will give you and then only if you pay extra, his tongue tasting of stale tobacco and whisky. I never imagined two men could kiss like that. Seems dumb now, but back then it came as a revelation of almost biblical proportions. My initial reaction was to pull back suddenly but I shut my conscience down and just went with it. My cock throbbed harder than it ever had before, multiplied tenfold by the fact my fingers burned like the buzz that's in the air during a lightning storm because they were wrapped around Colton's own hard cock. It felt so right, so natural, I knew I would never truly go back to the man I had been.

Colton pulled back for a moment. "Use your tongue, boy."

I'd only ever kissed a few whores like this and then it had been for practice for when I went a-courting to marry some respectable girl as I'd been told was the way. Now I knew there was another and I threw myself into it willingly. I thrust my tongue between Colton's lips with such force I almost choked him. He pulled away, letting go of my cock which was drizzling from the slit. "No need to go at it like a bull at a gate. Sure, that's good sometimes, but show a little tenderness, eh?"

So it was Colton taught me step by painstaking step, taking me from kissing, which I really liked, to the next step a few weeks later when he dropped to his knees and engulfed my hard prick in his warm mouth. I thought I would faint with pleasure. When he swallowed my load, I knew I had to try taking a man's cock in my own mouth. This wasn't just about me getting pleasure but about giving pleasure to my partner. Sinking to my knees, I took Colton's prick in one hand so that I could stare at its shape. I'd never really looked at another man's privates up so close and personal like. I liked it. The power I felt throbbing between my fingers. Tentatively, I leaned in to lick the hard gristle that was thicker and longer than my own. It tasted good: masculine and dusty like the man himself.

A thin pearl of cum oozed from the slit and I wanted to taste him badly but, at the same time, worried that it might not be to my liking. I worried unnecessarily because the moment Colton's flavor burst on my tongue, I was hooked. I can't say it rivaled the best of what Yan served us up as an evening meal but it came mighty close. I licked the hard prick from top to bottom, rewarded with heaving panting from Colton. "Lick my nuts," he pleaded. He had a hairy ball sac that smelled of sweat and hard work. I sucked each nut into my mouth, careful not to put too much pressure on them, until his scrotum was awash with my spit, then I returned my attention to his prick. I wanted to suck the essence out of him, just like he did me.

Colton was patient, guiding me through my initial attempts which must have been painful until I learned to keep my teeth out of my technique. Sure, I choked a few times when his enthusiasm outstripped his concern for my amateur status, but slowly I learned to please him. My crowning glory was the first time I managed to bring him off with my mouth without him flinching even once. I guess I passed my oral test.

By the end of my first cattle drive I was an experienced cocksucker and I was keen to try my new-found expertise on other horny men. Colton wanted for us to be a couple but I never heard of two men shacking up like a man and a woman and at my young age I couldn't see it was possible. Oh, he had stories about such men, mainly in the cities where they could hide in plain sight but out here on the prairies it was a different matter. Besides, he'd already sowed his wild oats whereas I was just getting started. It was unfair but that's how life is. We parted company with bad feeling on both sides although I'll always be grateful he opened me up for new experiences, taught me most of what I know about how to please a man. Last I heard he'd headed farther West with a group of likeminded men looking for some land to set up an outpost of communal living free of women. But I wished the man no harm and hoped he'd find his dream although it sounded mighty like the stuff of fairy tales to me.

I must have been day dreaming because Jake coughed to get my attention. "You must get lonely, Sheriff, being a single man."

I did but that was none of Jake's goddam business. The man was staring at me in expectation. Ah, what the hell, it had been months since I'd had some hard lovin' and Jake was just my sort. Sad to say, as I got older I began to see the appeal of settling down with a 'someone' who knew my needs and cared for me. I don't get this 'love' thing that women and poets never shut up about, although a good friend wouldn't have been a burden in my life.

But Jake was just a passing fancy. "I was going to check in on the new reverend but I think I'll give him time to settle himself in his new home; let him sit awhile with his wife before I get acquainted. How about I walk aways with you to Miss Kitty's?"

"That's mighty neighborly of you, Sheriff. But Miss Kitty's girls are too soft for the likes of a rough man like myself. You get my drift?"

"Yes, Jake, I think I do." Just to be sure, I glanced down at his dusty wool pants that had seen better days and noticed the bulge at the crotch. "You seem to be packing."

Jake noticed the direction of my gaze, and smiled. "Would you like to frisk me, Sheriff?"

"Indeed, I would."

Miss Kitty and me got along famously. I left her and her girls alone except when a cowboy threatened trouble and, in return, she allowed me the use of one of her rooms when the occasion arose. After I first took up my position in the town she was wary of me until I'd come to her rescue when her clientele had become raucous from too long on the trail or else too much liquor in their belly. She offered one of the girls as payment – or a bribe – but I politely declined. After five or six attempts to lure me she gave it away and, instead, we settled into a friendship of sorts. She cottoned on to my preference one day when I was called in to break up a fight between one of her girls and a young cowboy whose virility she'd called into question when he couldn't get it up.

When calm was restored and the girl's dignity satisfied, I realized the young man's problem could not be solved with one of Miss Kitty's girls. The young trail hand looked at me with more desire in his eyes than he did at any of the women in the bordello. Now, Miss Kitty ain't no fool. She noticed the staring going on between the two of us and suggested, "Sheriff, why don't you take this handsome young man aside and help him to calm down. We don't want him to leave the premises unsatisfied. Why, that would be bad for business if word got around." She took the key that dangled around her neck. "Here, use my room. It's private. Come and get me if you need anything."

I shoved the young cowboy toward Miss Kitty's room because his behavior was still belligerent. As I unlocked the door to her boudoir, Miss Kitty called after us, "Sheriff. Be sure to lock the door. And just so you know, there are no peepholes in my room like there are in the others, so it's very private."

Once inside the room, with the door locked, the cowboy kept up his pretense until I roughly pulled his head down until our lips touched. He fought me but with little conviction. I grabbed his crotch and felt his stiff hard rod straining against his pants. "Did Miss Kitty do that to you or is it me?" I asked.

He groaned. That was all the acknowledgment I needed. I peeled his clothes off his slim body, muscled from the hard work on the trail, until he stood naked before me. It had been so long since I'd had the opportunity to indulge and even then it had been just a quick fumble in the darkened sheriff's office. "What's your name?" I asked kindly as he stood attempting to hide his excitement with his hands. He made no effort to escape.

He was trembling. "Cord, sir."

"Well, Cord, just relax. We ain't gonna do anything that you don't want. You want me to stop, you just say so. We got a deal?"

"Yes, sir."

"You ever been with a man before?"

"Not like this. I played about a bit, that's all." He seemed wary perhaps thinking I was trying to trap him.

"Women not to your liking, son?"

"They're very pretty…"

"But they don't make you hard like looking at men does."

I removed my vest and shirt, Cord unable to take his eyes off my hairy chest and belly. He seemed mesmerized as I unbuckled and unbuttoned my trousers, his breath deepening as I slowly shucked my unwanted underwear and pants, my cock bobbing up fiercely, glad to be free.

I swear he was staring at my cock so hard I thought he'd lift the skin off. He must have realized what he was doing and snapped his head up to look me in the eye, real fear registering on his face. When he saw I wasn't about to arrest him or harm him he backed over to the bed and sat, dropping his face into his hands, sobbing uncontrollably. "What's the matter with me?"

I didn't want to play nursemaid to a confused young cowboy but I did want to feel his naked body against mine so I finished taking off my clothes and my boots and sat beside him on the bed, soothing him as best I could until he dropped his head against my shoulder. I stroked his hair, running my fingers down the back of his neck and along his jaw line. He moved his lips toward me. I kissed him, holding him tight against my body, allowing my hand to graze his skin as

I sought out his prick. Once I wrapped my fingers around it, he gasped loudly but made no effort to flee.

I sank to my knees as he sat, legs apart, on the edge of the bed, his eyes as big as saucers. I wrapped my lips around his shaft which was already leaking fluid. He bucked at the feel of the warmth engulfing him, groaning loudly. I took a break. "This your first time?"

He panted. "Yes. Like this. Don't stop."

I smiled. "I have no intention of stopping. By the time you leave Miss Kitty's establishment today, I'll teach you everything you need to know, son. We got a deal?"

"Oh, yeah."

I was true to my word, and I was mighty sorry when a more mature Cord rode out of town the next day, but that was the life I'd chosen. Miss Kitty stayed true to her word, too, and as a result I made use of her premises whenever I needed a similar favor. In return a certain peace settled over her establishment because everyone knew I'd stand for no bullshit. My two-rooms off the jailhouse were not private enough to use for these sorts of assignation.

That's where I took Jake. While he bathed to clean the grime of the journey from his body, I made my rounds of the town to ensure everything was locked down tight. The town's respectable women had descended on the Rev. Payne, the saloon was busy but not so crowded that fights were likely to break out, and everything was running smoothly. I could afford a little time for myself. I had a quick wash in preparation for Jake and he joined me in Miss Kitty's room, much too florid and feminine for my taste, but I wasn't there to appraise her decoration. Jake and I had business to attend to.

We wrestled for supremacy although we both gave up our ass in the end. Jake first and then me. It had been a while since I'd allowed any man to shove his cock into my hole. It hurt. Not as bad as being gored by a steer but pretty close. The first time I thought I was gonna die. I'd given it to a lot of men before then, including Colton, but I'd never let anyone near my own ass. The man to take my cherry was a rough rancher who thought a young buck like me was easy pickings. He forced more liquor on me than I was used to and then came to my room during the night. I tried to fight him off but I was no match for him. He was rough and uncaring and I was sore for days after. It made me wonder why any man would welcome penetration although I'd met many who did.

It took an older and kinder man to introduce me to the gratification that came with the act. I've long since lost the memory of his name although not of his ability to get me to scream with desire as he plowed my ass, my legs resting on his shoulders as his smoldering eyes focused all his attention on my face. He played my body, especially my ass, like a piano player caresses the keys, only the tune he played was pleasure. That's what enabled me to gain as well as give pleasure to and from Jake until our lips were bruised with kissing and our cocks were spent, our balls drained of their juice.

I thanked Miss Kitty profusely for the use of her boudoir before heading over to the church to check up on Payne who I found surrounded by a gaggle of middle-aged women and younger virgins of marriageable age. Word had spread quickly that the reverend gentleman was a widder man. His wife's coffin was laid out in the parlor as an admonishment to the wives who were pushing their unmarried daughters into the limelight. Headstone had a scarcity of marriage-age men – at least the sorts of men these mothers found acceptable.

Payne seemed grateful for some time away from the constant babble of female voices when I took him aside. "Thank you, Sheriff. It's been a long journey. I'm quite tired."

"Would you like me to disperse the ladies in the kitchen?"

"Good heavens, no. Fatigue is no excuse for neglecting God's work. I pray for hidden reserves of strength in order to do my duty by the good citizens of this town. I'm sure God will supply me with the stamina to go on."

I made no comment because I had never seen God supply anything to the town.

"My first priority, of course, is to ensure my wife has a decent Christian burial."

"I hear she died on the journey to Headstone."

"She was never in very good health, Sheriff, but she was a stalwart soldier in the fight against evil. She was one of God's most formidable Christian warriors."

This talk of soldiers and warriors did not augur well for Payne's tenure in the town. "You'll find few battles in Headstone, Rev. Payne."

He raised his eyebrows. "Oh? I'm told there is a bordello above the saloon."

"They leave you folks alone and you leave them alone," I said. "It's taken years to get peace in the town and I'd like to keep it that way."

"Evil must be destroyed wherever we find it, Sheriff. Good people everywhere cannot turn a blind eye to a festering sore. It must be lanced, just as the saloon and the cathouse must be closed down. That is God's law."

I bristled but kept my voice calm. "It may be God's law, Rev. Payne, but it holds no sway in Headstone.

Here we abide by Haskell's law and that includes you as well as the folk over at Miss Kitty's. I want no trouble here. And I don't want you ending up like some of your predecessors who are buried up on Boot Hill."

"Are you threatening me, Sheriff?"

"No, I'm telling you how this town runs. Good day, Rev. Payne"

I knew at once this Bible thumper was going to upset the fine balance of the town.

I did attend his wife's funeral as a mark of respect. Few people turned out for it, apart from the women with daughters, and Payne remained stoic in the face of the internment of his beloved wife. If he grieved, he must have done it in private although his face looked as if he were permanently aggrieved.

I attended his first few Sunday sermons but I, too, was seen as marriage material and had a stream of young women vying for my attention. That, and the good reverend's tedious Christian posturing and his inflammatory language persuaded me to bail after a few weeks. His strident attacks on sin and perversion were localized within church circles for the first few months, almost as if he were marking out his territory, although he caused enough concern that the saloon and other like-minded establishments came to me to see if I could rein in some of Payne's more outrageous rhetoric.

It was three months to the day that things turned from bad to worse. I know, because it was the stage that brought in the catalyst that would change the town forever. I moseyed over to the coach as Jake began to unload the mail as well as his passengers and their baggage. It was mainly people returning from visits to relatives or to the larger cities dotted along the trail. Jake never took his eyes off me and I, naturally enough, thought he was in the mood for another tumble after he'd had his bath. Three months is a long time between intimate human contact.

What he had been waiting for was my reaction to the final passenger to alight. I guess my mouth dropped open because I heard Jake snicker. The reason for my surprise was the young man who stepped from the coach, blinking against the glare of the sun. It was hard to tell he was a man except by his clothes because his hair, worn long so that it hung down to his shoulders, framed one of the prettiest faces I had ever seen. Yet, there was a masculinity to him that belied his feminine looks. My prick itched in my britches.

He spelled trouble with a capital T. I stepped forward to suggest he get right back on the coach and head out of here as fast as possible – that Headstone was no place for the likes of him – but before I could open my mouth to speak he stumbled over his own feet and fell headlong into me, almost knocking me down. I put my arms out to steady him. He ran his attention from my boots, up my body, to my face in the most lascivious manner. A few men who'd witnessed the incident snickered. The young man with coal black hair and eyes the color of obsidian looked at me and smiled. He noticed the badge on my shirt. "Thank you, Sheriff. That was very clumsy of me." He held out his hand, and said, "Benedetto." He had an accent so I wasn't sure if he'd spoken his name or if it was a greeting in a foreign tongue. Either way, I was determined to see him leave the town as soon as possible. I was about to tell him so when a loud female shriek behind me stole my attention. I recognized Miss Kitty's voice, but I did not recognize Miss Kitty herself when I turned because her face was alight with such good humor, the like of which I'd never seen before.

"Benny," she screamed, throwing herself at the young man, who seemed equally as delighted to see her.

I was shunted aside as they hugged each other in a most cordial greeting. It was only after a rather unsuitable amount of familiarity what with kissing of cheeks and pressing of bodies that my presence was acknowledged.

"Oh, Benny, this is Sheriff Chance Haskell." Miss Kitty made the introductions.

"My pleasure, Sheriff. You are very handsome. I think I am going to like your town. I may even have to break the law just so you can punish me."

Jake led the guffaws and I turned sunset red.

"Don't tease, Benny, the Sheriff is a good man."

Benny licked his lips as he looked me over like I was a prize steer, "A very good man."

"Sheriff, this is Benedetto Pani."

I whispered so we would not be overheard. "What's he doing here?"

"Benny is my new cook. For the saloon and for me. I miss the food of my old country."

I'd known that Kitty was not born in America but her accent had suddenly become thicker around Benny.

"Get him back on the coach and out of here," I hissed. "He's nothing but trouble."

Benny pouted. "The Sheriff does not like me."

"It has nothing to do with whether I like you or not. You can't stay in Headstone."

Benny put his hands on his hips, demanding to know, "Why not? I hear American is a free country."

I appealed to Kitty. "Explain it to him please."

"Explain what?" she asked.

I suddenly had a thought. "He's not going to be working in the upstairs?"

Kitty smiled. "Now there's an idea."

"Kitty." I shuddered at the concept. I could just about keep the lid on the town with female whores on tap, but a male whore? Who in their right mind would even contemplate such a concept? Maybe in a big city.

They must have seen the appalled look on my face and decided they'd taken the joke too far, for Kitty squeezed my arm, "What Benny does in his free time is his own business, but he's here just to cook, Sheriff."

I relaxed visibly. "It still doesn't mean with a pretty face like his it won't be a temptation for some men. Provided they don't tar and feather him first."

Benny positively minced at my comment. "Did you just call me pretty? You sure know how to win a man's heart." His demeanor changed instantly and he snarled at me. "I give a man one chance, Sheriff. You've just had yours. Never, ever, call me pretty again. Understand?"

He turned and flounced off with Kitty, heading for the saloon. Jake joined me as we watched the two of them enter the bar, followed the sound of wolf whistles a short time later.

Jake read my mind. "That one is gonna be a headache."

I sighed in agreement.

The trouble, when it came about two weeks later, hit like a cyclone. A group of herders rode into town looking for work and looking to spend their cash. I'd been forewarned by telegraph that these guys played rough so I was as prepared as I could be. There had already been grumbles about the food being served up at the saloon since Benny had arrived. He called it spaghetti, the hungry cowpokes called it shit. That didn't faze the young Italian and certainly a few men didn't mind the alternative to their diet, but the majority did mind and were very vocal about it.

The Rev. Payne, always looking for an opportunity to drive a wedge into the community took to calling the foreign food the Devil's vittles. On this subject he managed to unite both sides of the town divide, to the extent Benny had to modify his menu and include old favorites although he that did not stop him trying to force his own food on reluctant cowboys. His ruse was to pretend, late in the evening he'd run out of anything but his spaghetti dishes. He had so many names for the different shaped spaghettis they made my head spin. They made others angry.

The night the herders came into town Benny tried serving up his 'national dish' as he called it. I'd tried it and it wasn't half bad. Just took a bit of getting used to, that's all. But these men weren't gonna give it time. They smashed their plates against the saloon bar, cracking the mirror, vehement in their dislike of the foreign slop. Miss Kitty sent one of her girls to fetch me and I entered the saloon through the back door just as the herders were yelling for the cook.

I have to give Benny credit; he strode out to confront the angry cowboys showing no fear. When he appeared, all hell broke loose. The catcalls almost outweighed the curses and the sarcastic whistles. The men looked him up and down like he was some strange animal. "Who the fuck are you?" one of the cowboys asked.

Benny put his hands on his hips – definitely not a good idea under the circumstances. "Benedetto," he said. The men were well on the way to drunk and any provocation was gonna lead to violence.

The leader of the group turned to his men. "Hey, meet Bernadette; she's the new girl in town." There were drunken howls of derision. The leader walked up to Benny, towering over the young Italian, and chucked him under the chin, raising his face to meet his eyes. I could see the muscles in the cowboy's cheeks working and, sure enough, a huge gob of spit lobbed onto Benny's face. Everyone in the bar was silent, awaiting the fight. Benny merely scraped the saliva onto his finger and sucked it into his mouth, suggesting that he was one mean cocksucker. The cowboys got the hint.

"I think we got ourselves one of them perverts here, boys."

I held back in the hopes it wouldn't develop any further and that, just maybe, Benny would learn his lesson and high-tail it out of town on the next coach. No such luck. The leader decided to take the joke to the limit. "You like putting things in your mouth, pretty boy?"

I tensed. Sure enough, Benny said calmly, "I give you that one but it comes with a warning. Don't every call me pretty boy again. Understand?"

"Or what? You'll suck my cock? Well get to it, pretty boy."

The cowboy began to unbuckle his belt at the same time pulling Benny's head down toward his crotch. I was half way across the saloon when Benny struck, grabbing the cowboy's fingers and breaking them in one deft move, while kicking him squarely in the balls with his heavy boots. The cowboy went down screaming. His buddies joined the fracas and jumped Benny before I could get to him.

It was nine men against two of us because no one in the bar was gonna join Benny's fight. We put up valiant resistance, taking down six of them. Benny was a good fighter and surprised not only me but the men who attacked him, so much so that the three remaining were wary and stayed just out of reach. I'd lost my gun in the fight so Benny and I were back to back when the last three launched themselves at us. We both got the worst of it and looked like we were going down when a shot stopped us all in our tracks. Miss Kitty stood at the top of the stairs, smoking pistol in her hand.

"Next man makes a move on Benny or the Sheriff gets a bullet in their balls." No one moved. She addressed the three cowboys. "Get your men and get out of here. If you ever come back, I'll make sure you leave with your testicles in your coat pocket and your voice an octave higher. Understand?"

The men nodded.

"Now get out and take that other rubbish with you."

The men scrambled to obey, helping their buddies who couldn't help themselves, the others limping or holding their bloody heads in pain. They cleared the saloon in record time. Miss Kitty came down to examine the damage while I retrieved my gun from the barman who had placed it out of harm's way, wiping the blood from my eyes with the back of my hand. Kitty turned Benny's face to the light. He was as bloody as the image of myself I saw in the mirror behind the bar. "You'll live," she said to Benny. "Get upstairs and I'll have a hot bath made up for you. Tell Celine to prepare two. Looks like the Sheriff could use one as well."

There was a lot of blood but it came from a few cuts and abrasions. I was sore but nothing life threatening.

"Here," she said. "Try this." She poured me a good two fingers of whisky and I downed it in one gulp. It burned good on the way down and stopped the throbbing in my head. After I'd cleaned up, I went home and slept through until morning telling my deputy to wake me if there was any more trouble.

Payne attempted to stir up the incident by describing me as a defender of perverts but the town was very much on my side, even some of his congregation who didn't want to upset the peaceful town that I'd managed to create. The worst that came out of the incident was Payne's insistence on using the name Bernadette. It started being picked up by the less friendly men in the town. I knew I had to keep a lid on it.

The following week was pretty quiet, my one fear being that the cowboys would return for revenge. It never happened. So I went over to Miss Kitty's for my weekly bath. She was no competition for the town baths as she had set up mainly for the girls and the clientele who were always in need of a good soak. I'd got into the habit of using her premises in order to avoid talking town business with the men who went to the other establishment. Besides, Miss Kitty kept her premises in better condition. And the water was hot enough for my liking.

I soaked the week's activity out of my bones, the cuts and bruises from the fight almost gone. When the water cooled, I rang for more hot water to prolong the good feeling in my body. I had no modesty from the girls who worked there and Miss Kitty had given them instructions not to try anything. I was pretty proud of my cock, whether soft or hard, and many of the girls had commented on how big it was. I didn't mind flattery no matter where it came from.

"Come in," I called to the timid knock on the door as I lay my head on the back of the tub. I felt the new influx of hot water flood the bath from my feet up until the heat lulled me into semi-consciousness from which I awoke with a start when I felt a hand around my cock. "My, you do have a big one," a voice said.

"What the fuck…" I was usually on my guard but Miss Kitty's was a safe haven so I'd learned to let go. Stupid.

I pushed Benny away. "What do you think you're doing?"

"I was thanking you for coming to my aid last week. I've not had a chance to speak to you since." He looked at my cock which was so hard it hurt. "I can help you with that."

"I don't need your sort of help," I snapped churlishly. It was all too obvious that I did. But I'd do that alone in the privacy of my own room.

"Why? Because you don't do it with other men or you don't find me to your liking."

Before I could answer, he began to remove his clothes until he stood naked and magnificent before me. He was one of the best-looking men I had ever seen. I groaned.

"I know you're like me," he purred as he moved closer.

I snorted at the very idea.

He smiled. "You don't think so?"

I snapped. "No, I don't." I hadn't meant to be so abrupt.

He sat on the edge of the tub, running his fingers provocatively through the water without touching my skin. "You prefer the company of men. I'm a man."

I just couldn't let it be. "The jury's out on that."

Benny didn't seem upset by my nasty comments and if his cock was any indication – he was all man.

His fingers skidded across my chest, tangling in the hair, brushing across my nipples which made my cock twitch. He trailed his nails across my ball sac until my cock throbbed with longing. I flinched hoping he would leave me be or else get on with it.

"You must be lonely," he said.

"It's a cowboy's life," I replied.

"It doesn't have to be that way."

"What are you suggesting?"

"We could become partners."

"Partners? How?"

"We could take care of each other's needs," he said, gripping my cock and pumping it until I had to tell him to stop otherwise I would have lost my load.

"You want this to last?"

"God, yes."

I gave in. There was no point fighting it. Benny kneeled next to the tub, took a deep breath, thrust his head under the water, and buried his lips around my cock, sucking me all the way in until I felt his throat gripping my knob. I wriggled in the tub until it overflowed as I'd never felt anything like his hot mouth before. I held the back of his head as he made love to my cock. When he finally came up for air I was so close. He must have known because he stood and aimed his prick at my mouth. "Your turn."

I opened up and he pushed in. It wasn't the best angle at which to do it and I wasn't as accomplished as he was but I still managed to get little whimpers of appreciation out of him. That pleased me more than it should have. I glanced up at his face as I took his cock as far into my mouth as I dared. He was watching me, seemingly fascinated by the sight of his cock parting my lips. Even with his wet hair hanging like black spaghetti all over his face he was magnificent. I felt the clutch in his balls signifying he was close. I held his butt in place, increasing my rhythm on his cock until I felt him flood my mouth with his seed. It tasted salty. It tasted masculine. It tasted of Benny. He shuddered the last drops onto my tongue before pulling his sensitive prick from my mouth.

"That's not fair. I wanted it to last," he complained.

"Oh, I'm not finished with you yet."

I stood, the water cascading off my body, and stepped out of the bath. I enveloped him in my arms and kissed him with enough passion it would have reheated the lukewarm water. He molded his body against mine, digging his fingers into my butt cheeks as I fought to get my thumb into the puckered hole of his anus. At the same time our tongues fought for supremacy, my tongue in his mouth until he pushed back into mine. I didn't mind at all. That's one of the things that appealed to me about men: they fought back.

Taking him by surprise, I spun him around, pushing him down over the tub. He held on to the rim as I grabbed one of the sweet-smelling bath oils used by the whores, drizzling it on my fingers and over his crack until it covered his tight little hole. I pushed my finger inside. He tensed but eventually relaxed as I pushed in and out, opening him up. Then a second and a third finger until he spread his legs even wider in invitation. I oiled my cock and pressed against his bud, pushing slowly until the head brushed aside the muscle and was in. I stopped to allow him time to adjust. He nodded when he was ready and then inch by inch I sank inside him until my skin touched his.

"Oh, God, you feel so good," he panted. "Even better than I imagined."

I started to thrust slowly because I had never fucked an ass as good as this before. "You dreamed about me, did you?" I chuckled.

"Ever since that first day I fell into your arms."

I wasn't about to admit that I'd used my memory of him to fuel my solo sessions in my room. He just wasn't my type. Tell that to my cock.

"If I can't call you pretty, can I call you beautiful?"

"You think I'm beautiful?"

"You are without a doubt the most handsome man I have ever seen."

He turned his head and attempted to kiss me but the angle was wrong.

"I want to watch you as you fuck me," he pleaded.

I pulled out to lie the towels on the floor. He lay on his back, hoisting his legs almost to his chest to reveal the little brown bud that my cock yearned to plug. As I sank into his rectum, I brushed the stray hairs from his face, leaning over to kiss him, feeling his reawakened cock hard against my belly. I took it slowly at first until I could feel my balls churning then I picked up the pace slamming into him, mashing his body against the floor. He took every ounce of punishment I meted out, his ass gripping my cock as if he wanted more.

I put my hand over his prick, pumping it as I thrust toward completion. Benny shot his load first, his ring gripping my weapon, milking it until I shot deep inside him. I sank on top of him, his seed coating my stomach and my chest until we were stuck together. I was reluctant to move but I was heavier and I didn't want to crush him. I rolled over pulling him with me until he lay on top. He traced his finger across my face, me snapping my teeth at him as if I were an alligator.

"Come to my room?" he pleaded.

I was in no mind to turn him down. I grabbed my clothes and he led us both naked through the hallways to his room which he'd decorated in very masculine style. It was not at all what I'd expected. We lay under the blankets and fell into an exhausted sleep, waking hours later to repeat what we'd done in the bathroom.

"You know I want to fuck you?" he whispered.

Before I could stop my mouth from saying it, I muttered, "Next time."

His eyebrow arched. "There's going to be a next time?"

"I hope so," I said, my cock running away with my mouth. This was far too dangerous. It was okay to hitch up with Jake or an itinerant cowboy just passing through but Benny lived in town. Worse, he was so obvious.

We kept it discreet. Once a week on bath day, Benny and I would enjoy a tub together and then adjourn to his bedroom. I usually left the deputy in charge so I could spend the night if Benny wanted it. He always did. So it was I fell in love. I never knew such a thing was possible between two men. We played it carefully but it was foolish to think we could ever get away with it.

Payne's campaign against 'Bernadette' and the so-called sins and perversions that supposedly ran rife in the town because the sheriff looked the other way was beginning to have results. Payne's congregation couldn't let things be, he had to precipitate a full-scale confrontation. The girls at the saloon were getting nervous because some Christian women had taken to calling them whores in the street or else spitting at them. I begged Payne to curb his vitriol and to keep his congregation in line. He gave me a half-hearted promise that he would after I warned him of the consequences to the town and to him personally if the cowboys who used Miss Kitty's decided to get their revenge at the instigation of the girls. But he didn't keep his word; in fact, he fanned the flames.

He began insinuating that I was protecting Miss Kitty's and the saloon because I was a frequent user of the women and on the take from the bar. As long as he didn't hit on the truth, I let it be. Benny seemed impervious to all that was going on around us just as I was falling ever more deeply under his spell. I knew he liked me because he kept begging me to go away with him. I just couldn't see me pulling up roots to settle down somewhere with another man. It was all a dream.

The dream burst when Payne finally got himself a victory of sorts. One of Kitty's girls was so terrified by his preaching about hell and damnation she crossed over to the other side. And with her conversion and a quick marriage to one of the congregation's widowers, she revealed everything she knew about the whorehouse. The news that Benny and I were lovers capped it all off.

Payne ranted from the pulpit. I told Benny to deny it but he merely shrugged. "Why should I? It's true."

"It may be true but the folks around here are not likely to let it lie. At the very least they'll run us both out of town. At worst, they'll lynch us." But nothing would sway Benny, not even the intervention of Kitty who could see the end in sight and was preparing to up stakes and move her litter farther West where the likes of Payne had as yet not penetrated. I thought she was sensible in her attitude but Benny insisted we stay and fight.

Not only did the good Christian folk now call 'whore' at Kitty's girls they now turned their attention to 'Bernadette' and eventually to me, cursing and spitting as I walked by. They were not too proud, however, to call on my help when they needed it. The hypocrisy is what got to me. I began to plan my escape, wiring my money to a bank in a town farther along the trail, keeping just enough for a quick getaway.

Then Payne went too far. It was a Sunday service like any other. He was preaching fire and brimstone and the evils of sodomy although my guess is the good people of the congregation had no idea what sodomy actually involved. Just as well. That particular Sunday he stooped so low as to accuse Benny's mother of being Satan's whore. When it was reported back to me by one of the worshippers I'd planted as a spy, I had to act.

After the service I went to the church to confront Payne to tell him if he didn't tone down his language I'd be forced to run him out of town. He laughed in my face. A number of his parishioners hissed at me, people I had known for years and at whose tables I had supped. They treated me now as less than human. I warned Payne one last time but it had little effect and the following week he went further in vilifying me, Miss Kitty and her whores, Benny, and particularly Benny's mother.

Patronage had already fallen away at the saloon and bordello, cowboys preferring the comparative calm of the next town over. Those men who remained treated me with disdain, scarcely containing their contempt whenever I walked by. There was no way I would be able to control any situation in future. Even my deputies resigned in disgust. Miss Kitty had been sending her girls on by coach each week until only a skeleton staff remained.

I withdrew the last of my savings from the bank and ensured my horse was ready to go at a moment's notice. I had another saddled and ready for Benny. I may not have bought into his dream but I wasn't about to leave him behind. After the news of Payne's latest slander on my character I went over to the saloon to persuade Benny to come with me. If he wouldn't come voluntarily, I'd hogtie him and kidnap him but when I got to the Lazy Steer, the barman informed me that Benny had gone up to the church to have it out with Payne.

I ran as fast as I could because Payne had taken to wearing a gun – even in church – as a precaution, he said, because the spawns of Satan were out to get him. I didn't like the chances of an unarmed Benny against the rabid reverend. When I got to the church, Payne and a few of his followers were arguing loudly with Benny. I noticed to my distress that Benny, too, was wearing a gun.

"You will withdraw your remarks and apologize," Benny demanded. "I don't care what you say about me but when you impugn my mother's reputation, then you've gone too far."

"The sodomite comes to demand of me, the vicar of God?"

"You're no more a man of God than the whores who have fled the town. You're a fraud and I can prove it."

Payne laughed loudly.

"You know who my mother is that you so roundly condemn?"

"Some slut who opened her legs to any man she met in the streets?"

Benny kept his temper. Proudly puffing his body to its full height, he told Payne's congregation, "My mother is the Countess Maria Theresa di Medici." The name meant nothing to the congregation although they registered the word 'Countess' and seemed impressed, looking to Payne for a response. They were confronted with a minister who had turned ashen.

"Impossible," Payne croaked although he sounded very unsure of himself. "She has no children."

Benny continued to address the minister's followers. "The Rev. Payne is no servant of God, he's a common criminal whose real name is Horace Thurman. He's wanted up and down the East Coast for a series of daring robberies, especially from my own mother whose collection of jewelry and cash he stole. I have been tracking him for the past year to reclaim what was taken. The Sheriff will confirm this as there is a reward for his capture, dead or alive, and the return of the stolen goods."

"Don't believe this sodomite. He and the Sheriff are in this together."

"If you would care to accompany us to the jailhouse, I'm sure you'll find a wanted poster in one of the drawers with your likeness on it, Thurman."

Payne must have thought that attack was the best defense. "Your mother's material wealth is to be used for the glory of God. He asked me to take it from dissolute people like her in order to spread His gospel."

"You're such a hypocrite, Thurman." Benny half turned and Payne went for his gun. Members of his congregation screamed distracting me and I was slow in going for my weapon. Benny, however, was not. I had never seen anyone draw with the speed with which he had his gun in his hand. He fired before Payne could even raise his weapon. Payne fell, a red spot spreading across his chest.

"Now if no one minds, I will turn this church and Horace Thurman's rooms inside out while I look for my mother's jewels. Any objections?"

There were none so I headed back to the jail to see if I could confirm Benny's story. Yes, buried in one of the drawers of my desk was a wanted poster with a fairly accurate drawing of Payne or Thurman or whatever his name was. I strode back to the Church, pinning the poster on the front door with my sheriff's badge. Payne's followers bowed their heads in shame unable to look me in the eye and slowly drifted away.

Hearing the sounds of destruction inside the church, I entered to see a frustrated Benny overturning everything in his path.

"Nothing?" I questioned.

He whirled around, his gun already out of his holster and aimed at my heart, before I could get the words out. "I'm on your side."

"Did you find the wanted poster?"

"It's nailed to the door of the church."

"Then you're not here to charge me with murder?"

I laughed. "Even if you'd made the whole story up, I still wouldn't have charged you. It was a fair fight. He pulled his gun on you first."

"It's not here," he said miserably. "I've searched everywhere."

"I'm sorry, you must be…" I didn't finish the sentence.

Benny looked at me. "What were you going to say?"

"Damnation," I squealed. "I think I know where he's hidden it. Come with me."

We raced out of the church ready to sidestep Payne's body but it had been taken away by some of his admirers leaving the blood pooled on the stone entrance. We ran to the stables where we collected the two horses I'd prepared for our escape. If I was correct in my assumptions we'd have no need to return. Outside town we turned north, heading for the cemetery. I'd taken the precaution of grabbing a shovel when we left.

We arrived at the forlorn graveside of Anna Payne, marked by a simple white wooden cross with her name painted on the bar. "If I'm correct, the stolen goods are buried in this grave. I always thought it suspicious that Payne brought his wife's body with him even though he had a death certificate from a doctor from one of the town's along the coach route."

"Probably paid handsomely for it," Benny said, grabbing the shovel from me to begin the laborious task of retrieving the coffin.

There was little I could do but wait my turn at digging so I kneeled to watch as Benny shoveled dirt like a madman. I took over when it appeared he was ready to drop from the heat and he relieved me when we were almost to the coffin. I squatted, wiping my eyes to watch as Benny dug until the shovel made a dull thud as if it had hit wood. His energy didn't flag as he tore away the remaining inches of soil to reveal the coffin, prizing open the lid open with the shovel edge. There was no Mrs. Payne inside. What had been buried, however, were four bags which I surmised contained cash and jewelry. Benny kneeled to open one to display its contents to me. I whistled and then lowered a rope so Benny could tie the bags before I hoisted them to the top. I untied them and was about to drop the rope for Benny when I heard a gun cock behind me. I went for my own weapon which lay in the soil. A bullet ricocheted off a rock near my hand.

"I wouldn't if I were you," a voice cold as death advised.

I recognized Payne. "I thought you were dead."

"Very nearly," he said. "But it's God's will that I survived. God told me to let you dig up the stolen goods to save my strength. Please be as good as to join your partner. I will do you the honor of burying you both together so you'll be that much closer to the flames of hell. In you go."

I could see no way out, so I jumped into the open grave, barely missing Benny.

"Oh my God," Benny yelled. "There another two bags of my mother's stolen jewelry here." Benny signaled that I should crouch and block my ears. Fortunately, Payne was greedy enough to come to the lip of the grave. Benny shot him through the neck and he pitched forward, the two of us breaking his fall.

It wasn't difficult for us to clamber out. We loaded up the horses before pushing the soil back into the grave and stamping it down. The wind would do the rest until, in a matter of hours, there would be no indication the grave had ever been disturbed.

I swore when I remembered the reward for Thurman's capture, dead or alive.

Benny laughed as he mounted his horse. "Come on. We don't need it."

I followed behind; watching Benny's ass in the saddle and my cock ached.

He headed west. "Hey, New York is that way," I said.

He turned to smile at me. "So it is."

"You're not really related to the Countess at all, are you?"

"Nope," he laughed.

"Where are we going?"

He pointed West. "Our future is that way."

HE WON'T SEND ROSES

Just when I thought the day couldn't get any worse, the door to my florist shop opened and I knew I was going to die: stabbed, strangled, knifed, or shot. At that precise moment I wasn't sure which method he'd use, I only knew I was taking the last few breaths of my short and miserable life.

Why, oh why, hadn't I taken those self-protection courses the Gay Center ran on five consecutive Friday nights? *Why?* Because I'm too chicken shit, that's why. I was afraid of being laughed at by the gay men who attended the courses. That's what I told my friends when they encouraged me to be more pro-active. Pro-active? That sounded more like an ingredient you'd find in yoghurt to me. In private, I admitted to myself that the reason I wouldn't go to classes was a fear of failure, but also a fear that I'd be so turned on by the instructors and the other macho men in attendance I'd be crippled with desire.

But even now, confronted with my own grisly demise, I wasn't about to break out into a chorus of that Edith Piaf classic, "Je ne regrette rien" because, in fact, I regretted just about everything in my fucking life. If I was one of the Seven Dwarfs, my name would be Timid.

Thirty years old and afraid of my own shadow. Qualified for nothing, although I'd taken my uncle's florist shop, *Petals to the Metal*, from near bankruptcy to a thriving business. I don't have a head for big business; my life comes in smaller portions. I don't really have a body for small business either. Those long hours on your feet, fighting with pushy sales people, screaming about missing deliveries, trying to keep an eye on the shady shop assistants – mainly drunks and drug addicts – the sort of people who respected my uncle but who see me as an easy mark.

My uncle believed in attempting to rehabilitate society's downtrodden. He liked to give everyone the benefit of the doubt, give them one chance to redeem themselves. He was a true humanitarian. Even when someone he trusted turned out to be a thief, absconding with the day's takings, he would shrug and say, "Poor bastard, he probably needs it more than I do."

I guess I was one of those 'poor bastards' because he took me in when I turned up on his doorstep one miserably cold night. Too timid to knock because it was after midnight even though I knew Uncle Ben lived above the shop, I huddled down in the doorway, drawing my legs up to my chest in an attempt to keep the chill winter wind out of my bones. I pulled my threadbare coat around my torso and buried my hands in my armpits. My beanie protected my ears. That's how Uncle Ben found me the next morning when he opened the shop.

"What on earth? Christopher." He hoisted me up from the cold front step; the newspaper I'd folded under me having failed to keep out the cold, my ass was as numb as my face after a visit to the dentist to have a tooth pulled. He hugged me tightly in an attempt to warm me up but when he realized it was a losing battle and that my teeth were chattering, he took me upstairs and, once he'd help me remove my meager wardrobe, shoved me under the warm spray in the shower.

It had been more than a week since I'd bathed and I must have smelled rank. I couldn't control the shakes so my uncle held me as he soaped my back with a soft sponge and a lavish smelling liquid soap before turning his attention to my hair. I was too tired and hungry to care that my uncle had seen me naked. In fact, was innocently running his hand all over my body, including my privates, which until then had been seen by few enough people. When he'd finished and rinsed me off, he wrapped me in the most luxurious towel I had ever felt.

Back home, rough and threadbare were good enough for my father. Anything else was a waste of money and would certainly lead not only to penury but a short-cut to Hell. I guess my mother must have agreed with him because she'd married the bastard. She must have agreed with him as well when he called me a 'foul tool of Satan' and 'a blight on the family name.' All because he'd discovered a magazine I'd hidden in my room. I had a special hiding place under the floorboards for my small stash of personal items because I knew he searched my room while I was out. I must have been careless or else he had better tracker dog senses than I gave him credit for, because that day when I came in from late afternoon chores he was seated at the family table, his Bible open, mouthing the words of some Psalm or whatever it was he had been instructed was appropriate for the occasion.

I doubt that Jesus had much to say about copies of *Big Cocks & Gaping Assholes Issue #34.* I suppose it might have gone marginally better for me if the 'gaping assholes' in question and in glorious full color had been female. But they weren't. They were juicy plump men's butts. He laid into me with his belt. I'd become almost immune to it by this stage but he was particularly vicious that night. He was trying to beat the wickedness out of me. I know because he told me. My mother sat at the table, her eyes downcast as if the pattern of grain in her dining table was of more importance than her son.

I was sixteen years old, nothing in the way of 'real-life' experience, and I still didn't have the guts to stand up to my old man. He was big man, over six feet tall, while I was a stripling, barely making five foot seven inches, and about a third his weight. He could have crushed me like a peanut if I'd fought back. The only way I'd ever defeat him was with a gun, and I abhorred violence. My resistance was passive. I did a Gandhi. I would never give him the satisfaction of begging him to stop, or of crying. It was simple. I left my body. It was a poor enough vessel and it would pain like the devil in the morning but each stroke of his belt merely fortified my resistance.

I'd saved a little money, but not enough. It lay on the table, spilling out of the rusty tobacco tin in which I'd hidden it. It had been in the same spot as my precious magazine. I was sent to bed with no supper, my bedroom door locked to prevent my sneaking downstairs to the refrigerator which would have done Old Mother Hubbard proud. My bedroom window had long ago been barred, to prevent burglary I'd been told, but the house contained nothing of value. In fact, my small treasure trove was probably worth more than most everything else in our home. We weren't poor by any means; my father was merely parsimonious. He justified it from the Scriptures.

That night I lay in bed listening to my father discussing my life on the other side of the wall. He either didn't realize his voice carried, or else didn't care, for I heard every word of the discussion. Not exactly a discussion because he was telling my mother what he was going to do with me.

"The Church is getting amazing results with this, what do they call it? Here it is, Reparative Therapy. They guarantee results. Listen here, 'In a matter of months we turn the most intransigent perpetrator of unnatural acts into a follower of the message of the Lord Jesus Christ. With no expense to you'."

I could almost hear the glee in his voice at that last bit.

"Will Christopher have to go away?" my mother asked meekly.

"It's for his own good. Otherwise he is damned."

I heard her sigh.

"The Reverend Stadler will call in the morning and transport him to the Correctional House where he'll be a guest until the cure takes."

My mother was skeptical. "I don't know. Christopher can be very stubborn when he sets his mind to it."

My father snorted. "They'll soon beat that out of him. They have all the modern techniques at their disposal. It says here they even use electricity to shock the unnatural behavior out of the sinner."

I'd read about electro-convulsive therapy on the internet at the town library when I first realized I had no hankering for the female of the species and that I was right excited by the male. For a few weeks, I'd considered myself an 'abomination.' I'd heard the word often enough vomited from the mouth of Rev. Stadler during one of his boring Sunday sermons in the small wooden church in our town. I guess repetition does something to your self-esteem; it did to mine. I started to explore the internet to see if I could change. That's when I'd stumbled across various organizations that 'guaranteed' they could turn you from gay to straight with the help of prayer, and a little electricity, a little light beating, a little cruel training, or a little aversion therapy that included a lot of puking. I'd also discovered that the process didn't work.

Knowing it was just a matter of time before my secret was discovered – my father was already hinting that he would look favorably on any girl I brought home – I was making plans to escape, hoarding any small scrap of cash I could find or earn. With nowhere to turn, I'd listened to the odious comments my father made about my mother's brother, my Uncle Ben. I'd managed to track him down via the computer in the library, and even managed to contact him via my secret email account. My father didn't hold with computers or anything remotely technological. I'd had no training with the machines which were as daunting to me as a flying saucer would be to people who'd never seen aircraft.

The librarian, Mrs. Pangborn, helped me any time I had a problem. I think she felt sorry for me because I'd been home schooled from the age of twelve. I guess she thought it was because I was slow. I was in some ways. I'm not stupid but I had little experience of the ways of the world.

I knew Uncle Ben was like me because I'd heard my dad describe him as a 'pillow biter' and other much more repellent names. "It must run in your side of the family," my father informed my mother the night he'd discovered my magazine. Ironic that my father was inadvertently admitting that homosexuality was in our genes rather than a 'lifestyle choice.'

Uncle Ben and I corresponded via email on an irregular basis. I revealed a little about my predicament but I didn't want to burden him with my problems. His emails were full of chatty anecdotes about his life thousands of kilometers away in a big coastal city. He had been guarded at first, but once I admitted, my heart beating fit to burst out of my chest as I typed tentatively with two fingers, that I was 'like him.' I'd backspaced almost a dozen times to delete the incriminating line – what if he wasn't like my father said? – until I took a deep breath, closed my eyes once the cursor was over the Send button, and clicked. It was the bravest thing I had ever done in my life.

Normally, I waited two to three days between visits to the library. I was ostensibly there to improve my mind with religious tracts and other books of similar values, all from the list provided by my father. Mrs. Pangborn had to sign off on the list whenever I borrowed a book, which she dutifully did. She would also slip me a book every now and then that most certainly would not have been approved by my father. "We're throwing this one out, Christopher. I think you might like it," she'd say in a whisper as if some great conspiracy was afoot. It's not that they were 'bad' books or anything like that; they were just normal books that nobody had wanted to read for quite a while and with shelf space at a premium, Mrs. Pangborn was forced to discard the old, neglected volumes. She sighed. "I do hate to throw away old books. I always like to see they go to a good home."

I couldn't keep them, of course, but once I'd read them under cover of darkness with a flashlight under my blankets, or lazing on the straw in the barn when I knew my father was in town or visiting neighbors, I mulched the pages in with the pig swill or else burned the hard covers in the barrel the family used for disposing of unwanted flammable matter. I was sorry to see them destroyed in this way but I had gleaned all I could from them, and my life, let alone Mrs. Pangborn's, would not have been worth living if my father had discovered them. He never did.

I had more immediate concerns on my mind that night. No matter how submissive my outward appearances, it was unimaginable that I would allow myself to be carted off passively to the horrors of whatever torture and humiliation the Church deemed necessary for my conversion and my so-called salvation. Over the years, preparing for an escape I saw as inevitable as death, I had loosened the bars on my window. Fearful, in case my father discovered I was white-anting his prison bars, I carefully removed any trace of my handiwork, prepping the bars to look as solid and immovable as, indeed, they had been in the beginning. Had he tested them with any strength, they would have come out of the window, revealing my plans.

I waited until I heard my dad's stentorian snoring which meant my mother would have inserted her ear plugs surreptitiously to avoid another confrontation with him. "Snoring is natural," my father insisted. "It's God's sign that a man has done a good day's work." In that case, ear plugs were the work of Satan, but if my mother was to get any rest at all, she'd have to move to another town out of earshot, or resort to using the Devil's tools. I, at least, had a wall separating us.

It was the longest half-hour I ever experienced, giving them time to sink into deeper torpor before I sneaked from my bed to the window which I'd opened when I went to bed without supper because it was old, and rattled. I had my Swiss Army knife which I'd persuaded my father was essential for me to use around the farm. He'd examined it minutely when I had first brought it home, perhaps because he feared it was a weapon I could use against him. Satisfied it would inflict minimal damage no matter how I used it, I was still surprised when he returned it to me.

I'd used it to cut grooves in the window sill. With the largest blade, I worked feverishly to clean out the small channels I'd disguised with shavings and glue and any spare putty I managed to secrete. I scored the channels deeper, always aware of time passing. I wanted to be long gone before sunrise when my father would get up to begin his chores. He'd knock on my door around 5am only to discover I was gone. I had no idea what his reaction would be: whether he would call out the sheriff, or the folks from his Church. Either way, if they caught up with me, I was fucked.

It was after midnight before I managed to bend the bottom half of three of the bars enough to shimmy through the opening. The jagged edge of one cut my skin and shredded the T-shirt I was wearing but I wasn't about to clamber back inside to retrieve another. I had little by way of clothes but I'd bundled up what I thought I'd need for my journey, packing them in my backpack which I'd tossed out the window ahead of me, listening for any change in my parents' bedroom after it thumped on the ground outside, then I'd followed.

This was the only time I was grateful my father was too miserable to keep a dog. No tearful goodbyes or snarling send-offs. I sneaked past the house, frightened that at any moment I would hear my father's voice stab through the dark, "Where do you think you're going?" My heart thudded so loudly in my chest I was sure it would wake him. But I reached the roadway in front of the house without bumping into any old items left scattered about the yard, and without being detected.

It was unlikely I would be able to thumb a lift along the dirt road which led into town and then on to the busy expressway. Even had I contemplated that escape route, it would almost inevitably have been someone from a neighboring farm who picked me up resulting in my being returned to the family in no time flat. I headed in the opposite direction; a more circuitous route but it would take me south of the town to the old highway that truckers used to avoid the toll on the new multi-lane expressway. I guessed my father, who had little imagination, would expect me to take the easier option which might mean a few hours head start.

I hurried along the miserable road to salvation, most of the asphalt long worn away, the town too cash-strapped to repair it, hiding among the bushes and long grass at the edge when a car or truck approached in the dark. Fortunately, I heard them rattle over the pothole-ridden track before I even saw the beam of headlights. It was much too dark to see me crouching only half concealed as they rode past.

Time was important. There was no chance to dawdle, so I walked faster as the hours ticked away until, with a last burst of speed, I emerged into the melee that was the old coastal highway. It was little used except for locals and truckers delivering goods between the major cities so I faded into the background to allow cars to pass and thumbed the air on the approach of a truck. It was still chancy and I wouldn't relax until I'd put some distance between me and my family, although I had already shifted a gear in my mind so that family equaled Uncle

Ben. If that didn't pan out, then I'd find another family, or another, until one that suited me.

I'm not callous, and I would miss my mother, but that was now the past. Had I known what the next few weeks had in store, I may have changed my mind. I was lucky to escape, still clutching desperately to my virginity but little else. It took ages to reach my destination, first with a sympathetic trucker who asked if I was running away from home but who merely shrugged when I lied, then with more predatory types including an old man, disturbingly like the Rev. Stadler, who put his hand on my knee and suggested that a fair payment for his providing a taxi service was that I service him. His lip was bleeding when he pulled over on the side of the road to expel me from his car with a series of curses.

I showered in trucker stop gas stations where I could, filched food from the dumper bins at the back of supermarkets in shopping malls, and slept curled up in rest areas in a futile attempt to keep warm. Along the way, the little that I had was stolen while I slept in a deserted shopping mall out of the wind and out of police view, but obviously on the criminal radar. So it was I finally arrived at Uncle Ben's doorstep, tired, hungry, stinking, and filth-encrusted. A few days later after a good wash (or three because there was grime in the most unlikely places), loads of sleep, a few good meals, plus a new wardrobe of clothes after Uncle Ben declared the rags I'd worn in my escape were toxic, I felt human again. It finally sank home, too, I was also an orphan of sorts.

I'd been in the room after I'd had my first bath when Uncle Ben rang my parents. The only reason they had a phone was because my father suffered from numerous medical complaints that sometimes necessitated an urgent call to the local ambulance service. It also came in handy when my asthma attacks threatened to overwhelm me although he usually left it until the very last moment muttering about the cost of medical treatment as if I had the attacks on purpose just to annoy him.

Uncle Ben rang to assure my parents I was okay – he didn't want to face a charge of kidnap – but it was a moot point because, after listening to the opening remarks about how I had arrived, my father replied, "I have no son," and disconnected the call. I'd heard because Uncle Ben had put him on speaker phone. He looked more devastated than I did. My reaction was "Good, I don't have to worry about them. Now I can get on with the rest of my life."

I soon settled into a pattern with my uncle's help, thriving under his tutelage. With the help of a high school teacher, Adrian, one of Uncle Ben's closest friends, the huge gaps in my education and my life experience were plastered over so that by the next school year they confidently enrolled me in a gay-friendly establishment where I felt at home for the first time in my life. I made friends and lost just as many until a few stuck. I experimented, had my heart broken on occasions so numerous that I would have to wrap it in sticky tape if it happened again, realized no one died from thwarted love, and generally did the sorts of foolish things a young adult does until he becomes aware that the universe doesn't revolve around his wants and needs.

So it was I grew into a fairly responsible adult ready to take his position in society although, courtesy of Uncle Ben and his radical friends, with a world view definitely leaning toward the progressive spectrum. Oh, how my father would have hated it. I admit that part of my embrace of unpopular causes was in reaction to my parents' fundamental conservative Christian view of the world, and a heaven I no longer believed in, but it also appealed to the basic decency that had somehow managed to survive despite the repressive regime in which I'd spent the first sixteen years of my life. Once nurtured by a group of adults who saw it as their duty to encourage independent thought and action rather than abide by a set of slavish rules, I flourished.

Through high school and college I worked in Uncle Ben's florist shop and so became familiar to the locals. I was a timid soul and many of them scared me. They were big and aggressive although my uncle always knew how to calm them down. He was a sucker for a sob story but hard as steel in his refusal if he thought they were lying or going to use his largesse for drugs or booze. His downstairs back rooms were often used for political meetings by groups who felt sufficiently marginalized that they needed to plan demonstrations or letter-writing campaigns. These same rooms were also a haven for women who just wanted a calm oasis from the daily grind of their lives and so would meet on an ad hoc basis to knit or sew or just generally gab.

The women were always attempting to pair me off with their daughters or nieces or granddaughters, always the wrong gender, until I moaned to Uncle Ben and he had a discreet word in their ears. Perhaps I should have left it alone because then they began on the 'boys like that' they knew in the neighborhood. Unfortunately, I'd had the majority of the men they mentioned, quick fumbles in their car or in a cubicle at a bar, because they weren't 'out' even though it sounded as if their secret was the worst kept in the history of the world. Mrs. Melito was the worst. An olde world Italian who still spoke with an accent as thick as pasta, she was forever going on about her nephew who she insisted would be my soul mate. He was the son of her brother and was a 'good boy at heart,' she insisted. That expression was enough to raise my concern. Was the subtext that he was a member of the Mafia? The Melitos were from Sicily.

Uncle Ben told me I was being racist. "Not all Sicilians are Mafia," he said. I knew that, it was just the manner in which Mrs. Melito spoke about her nephew. I had a vision of a guy the size of a thug with dark glasses and an assassin's bullet ready for anyone who got in his way. Fortunately, he was somewhere overseas attempting to find himself. I was hoping for a long and fruitless search so he'd remain where he was. I'd had enough of Mrs. Melito's match-making. In fact, everyone's interference in my love life. I had to make my own mistakes, like my ill-fated infiltration of the leather BDSM scene. Sure, the sight of a hot man in leather got my gonads churning, and I did like my sex rough on occasions, but allowing myself to be dominated, hog-tied and beaten was quite a few steps too far.

One of my extended family was always there for me if Uncle Ben was otherwise occupied with his grass roots campaigns for gay marriage, or against police profiling which resulted in a high proportion of non-Anglo Whites being stopped and frisked, or any of the myriad charities in which he was involved. It was an enchanted life for me and I thought it would go on forever.

When Uncle Ben had first opened his shop in the area it had been a predominantly middle-class area but with time it had become more run-down and squalid, attracting people lower on the socio-economic scale, including those who preyed upon people with big dreams and small incomes: drug pushers, loan sharks, stand-over merchants, and their runners. It was my uncle's ability to see good in everyone that was his undoing. He could not believe that Chet Marsh, local high-school hero who had thrown away his career for the fleeting high of heroin, would harm him the night Chet came seeking money for his habit. Uncle Ben had been like a second father to him, had even paid for Chet's first unsuccessful attempt at rehabilitation.

So the last thing Uncle Ben expected was the gun Chet pulled or that he would fire when my uncle refused to open the till and hand over the day's takings. The look of surprise on my uncle's face when I came out of the back room where I was tutoring some of the locals who had fallen behind in the high school work – an irony that was not lost on me – said it all. The look of horror on Chet's face revealed the enormity of what he had done. He flung the gun down and ran for it. I rang the cops after I rang for an ambulance.

Chet didn't get far; he was found sweating and cowering in one of the rooms of an abandoned apartment building used by junkies a mere three blocks away. The police report said he kept muttering over and over, "I didn't mean to hurt him. I'm so sorry." That did nothing to assuage my anger although Uncle Ben, critically ill in hospital told me "Tell Chet I forgive him." I didn't. You can think what you like about my hypocrisy but when I heard about Chet being killed in prison a few years later, I gave a little jig.

The last thing Uncle Ben said to me, three days after he was shot, me holding his hand as I sat beside his hospital bed, was "Take care of our shop, Christopher. It's important." Then a bank of machinery beeped loudly and gurgled although I'm pretty certain the gurgling sound was coming from me as I sobbed at the death of the only person I called family. I leaned over to kiss his cheek as nurses burst into the room, my tear-filled eyes blurring my vision as someone led me from the room.

The next two weeks were agony. I closed the shop although I kept the back rooms open for those who needed them. I had no interest in what was going on, only registering feebly the condolences that poured in by letter and email and in person. Uncle Ben had been a popular personality. Adrian took over the arrangements because I was gutted and of no use to anyone. Still, I was surprised the day I'd come downstairs to retrieve one of my books that my uncle had borrowed to read in the slow periods while at the counter to discover Adrian showing my parents over the shop.

They had their backs to me, so I heard my father saying, "I suppose something like this will fetch a pretty penny?"

"I imagine so," Adrian agreed. "Although I'm not sure it will be put on the market."

My dad seemed adamant that it would. "Our Church back home is in desperate need of funds to spread God's word, and what with my wife here being next of kin, I think a quick sale is in order."

Adrian looked surprised. "I'm not sure…"

They must have heard my movement as I walked into the shop because they all turned; my mother's face a picture of surprise. "Christopher," she said softly before my father elbowed her into silence. They must have believed I'd moved on from Uncle Ben's or else had met an equally grisly demise. My parents registered the change in my appearance. I had left their home a skinny runt of a farm boy; here I was six years later a confident man who had filled out and bulked up courtesy of better eating habits and regular exercise. I was considered quite a catch to the denizens of gay clubs although, when I looked in the mirror, I failed to see why.

My parents couldn't leave the shop quickly enough although my mother glanced over her shoulder from the doorway, a look of admiration and then sorrow flitting across her face. At least that's how I read it. Adrian apologized for their intrusion, knowing of my history. "They had to be invited," he said. "Your mother is his closest kin. Do you know what's in Ben's will?"

I didn't. "He was still a young man, I never thought to ask. Anyway, it was none of my business. All I know is he would be horrified if it went to those homophobes to spread more hate."

Adrian sighed. "I was always on at him about making his will, but I don't know if he did. We could always fight your parents if he didn't."

"I don't have the money to fight it," I said. "But I'd rather burn the shop to the ground than allow my father to get his hands on it."

The day before Uncle Ben's funeral, my father turned up with a real estate agent to give him an appraisal of the property's value. I'd been forewarned, explaining to Adrian that I didn't even know if my uncle owned the shop and land outright or whether he had a mortgage. No one as yet had found his papers. Or a will. My father's attitude was jubilation and I suspect he never stopped thanking God for His generosity.

He was still gloating the next day, heard to mutter "He'll be closer to Satan," as Uncle Ben's coffin was lowered into the ground. Fortunately, I was hemmed in by legitimate mourners on three sides otherwise I would have knocked him down. My parents stood apart from everyone else at the grave side as if the other mourners were contagious. They didn't attend the wake where Uncle Ben's life was celebrated. I almost wish they had because they may have learned what a good and gracious man he had been. I don't dare think where I would be today if it hadn't been for his kindness and understanding. He had been father, mother, friend, confidant, and hero to me.

Mrs. Melito had a glass of white wine and was balancing a number of sweet cupcakes on her plate when she found an opportunity to speak to me. "Wonderful service," she said quietly. "Apart from that miserable pair who stood apart like they'd catch cooties."

I smiled. "My parents."

She was unrepentant. "Ah, now I understand why you ran away."

I'm afraid I laughed. Uncle Ben would have liked that.

"I would have liked a mention of God but I know your uncle didn't go for that sort of thing," Mrs. Melito continued. "No matter. He'll be with the angels because that's what he was. An angel." I thought she'd finished her own personal eulogy, but she went on. "What will you do with the shop now?"

She, like many others, assumed that I would take control. "It's not that simple," I said. "It seems my uncle didn't make a will, so chances are a good portion of the estate will go to my mother, Uncle Ben's sister."

"He did so make a will," Mrs. Melito said in a voice loud enough to be heard by everyone in the room. "I was one of the witnesses."

Adrian hurried over and bundled Mrs. Melito to one side. It took a little time but Adrian tracked down the retired lawyer whom my uncle had used in an effort to help him out of penury and, indeed, after scrounging through his miniscule but untidy-enough-for-demolition apartment, the will retrieved and, eventually, probated.

My father reacted with such fury when he learned the news, I thought he was in danger of self-immolation. He and my mother waited around just long enough to hear they were not recipients of my uncle's estate but not long enough to hear his scathing condemnation of their behavior toward their son who received the bulk of Uncle Ben's small fortune. It was enough on which to live comfortably for the remainder of my life. He had not forgotten his friends and locals, many of them receiving small bequests. Adrian immediately donated his to a charity for homeless GLTBIQ youth. My father, however, sent me a bill for his extended stay in the city. I ignored it and heard no more.

I graduated college that year, not yet having made up my mind what I wanted to do with my life. Uncle Ben had encouraged me to pursue my dream – but, basically, I didn't have one. I realized, though, I had plenty of time to make a decision. The florist shop began to flourish as gay men moved into the depressed inner city area, converting old warehouses into open plan apartments, and renovating the old terrace houses into bright sparkly gay residences for gentlemen with no cash-flow problems.

I gussied up *Petals to the Metal* to the point I had a number of local unemployed motorcycle youths making deliveries. I learned which of them could be trusted and, a number with a fluid sexuality sensing a way out of what had been their ghetto lifestyle, began a lucrative sex trade on the side. I turned a blind eye to such activity unless it interfered with the business and, as a result, a number of young men escaped the economic deprivation in which they'd been raised. I'm not sure Uncle Ben would have approved of their methods as he frowned on prostitution. I'm of a more pragmatic bent.

So it was I sort of drifted into caretaker mode for the florist shop, adding DVD rental, a book swap section, a small internet section, and, finally, a coffee stand for early morning passing trade on their way to work. My sex life was pleasant, if underwhelming, consisting of short-lived affairs, and sexual experimentation on my part. I went to saunas and gay bars to relieve the itch in my groin, treating the occasions in much the same way I treated birthdays and Christmas. They were special and had little or no relationship to my everyday life. I'd achieved equilibrium; a sort of contentment. That's how eight years passed me by, until I found myself confronted with 'him.'

I knew he was trouble the moment he entered the shop. I was preparing the Valentine's Day floral tributes, cursing that the delivery man or woman was running late, totally alone as it was still too early in the morning even for my caffeine regulars. I was too trusting; I should have locked the door, not that the glass panels in the entrance would keep out a determined thief – or killer.

The door had one of those old-fashioned bells that jangled to let me know when someone came in. Looking up I was confronted with my worst nightmare. A giant of a man, a bandana wrapped around his forehead, otherwise dressed only in tight leather pants and biker boots. He was pierced and inked. He was a formidable fucker and my knees buckled. He glanced around the shop as if to scope out the enemy. I stood up from where I had been sorting dozens of red roses as I consulted my order list, and backed up against the counter keeping my hands where he could see them.

He eyed me up and down, his lips curling in a smirk that said he knew I was no threat. My life may be a little on the dull and uneventful side, but there was no way I wanted to die for the miserable few bucks in the till at the hands of some junkie who just wanted enough for his next fix. Shit, to save my neck I was prepared to go to the nearest ATM and take out as much as he needed. "Just take the cash and go," I squeaked in a voice so terrified it barely carried. "There's not much but it's all yours. Don't hurt me, just take it and go."

I'm not too proud to say I was on the verge of pissing in my pants. He just stared at me as if I were an alien with two heads, then threw back his head and laughed fit to burst. I failed to see the humor in my imminent disembowelment. The intruder laughed until he had tears in his eyes. I suppose I could have made a run for it but he was blocking an escape via the front door and although I could have locked myself in one of the back rooms and called the cops, this brute would have been able to break down the door in seconds flat. And the back door merely emptied into a yard bordered on three sides by the brickwork of adjoining houses and factories.

I regretted now that I hadn't taken Adrian's advice to buy myself a gun. There's no way I could have fired a weapon but I could have used it, unloaded, as a threatening prop to, perhaps, escape unharmed. What I did have was a pair of secateurs for pruning the roses. I grabbed it off the counter, holding it in front of me, the curved blade pointed at the intruder. I backed away from the till. "Go on, take the money and go. Just leave me the fuck alone."

The intruder appeared surprised although he didn't take that superior smirk off his handsome face. Handsome? How had I managed to scrutinize his good looks while terrified I was about to die smothered in his powerful, muscular arms? OMG! I was getting turned on by my own murderer. I really am pathetic.

I was ready to surrender to my fate when he went and got my temper up. "For God's sake, put those things down or you'll end up cutting yourself."

People tend to do foolish things when they're mad. I began to inch toward him, thrusting the pruning shears aggressively ahead of me. He was so fast I didn't even see him move. The end result was painful as he bent my arm behind my back, confiscating the dangerous weapon. He dropped it to the floor, kicking it behind the counter, then put his arm around my neck. I could smell his intoxicating, masculine odor; feel the warmth and power of his muscles against my neck. I relaxed into the death hug.

Make it quick, I prayed.

Instead of applying pressure, the guy let me go, taking a step back to just out of range of my fists. "I'm not here to rob you. Or hurt you. You must be Christopher."

The penny dropped. The agency had sent him to do the deliveries. He was late, but I felt an absolute fool. "Shit. I'm so sorry. I took you for a thief. Please accept my apologies." I wanted the earth to open up and swallow me.

"Apologies accepted. No harm done except to my ego. I'm pissed that you thought I was here to rob your store." He gave a little boy sulk which made me laugh.

I looked him up and down carefully. "I'm sorry, though. You just won't do. You're much too scary to deliver flowers in this neighborhood." He went to object. "Don't worry. You won't be out of pocket. I'll see to that. I don't know what the agency was thinking sending someone who looks like you."

"What do you mean, looks like me?"

"You're too…threatening. You're too big." I wanted to add, *You're much too good looking, the gay men around here will eat you alive. Or die trying.*

"I'm a pussycat," he said making an unsuccessful attempt to look coy.

"I'm sorry. I really am." Besides, I'd find eye candy like him much too distracting. "If you'll pardon me, I have to ring the agency and get someone else. I'm snowed under."

He seemed more amused than dejected that I was rejecting him. I didn't want to. He was my ideal man, but men who looked like him never gave me the time of day. They sneered at a wimp like me. Getting too close to their supernova of looks and masculinity would only result in getting burnt. But, oh, what a lovely way to burn.

"Okay, I can take a hint. Thanks, anyway."

I don't know what he was thanking me for. He made his way back to the front of the shop and I couldn't take my eyes off the way the black leather clung to his chunky ass. My tongue poked out between my lips, eager to get down and worship him all over. He must have sensed my stare because, on the threshold, he turned and winked. "See ya."

As soon as I came back down to earth and adjusted my stiffening cock in my trousers, I rang the agency. Of course, being early in the morning, the sun still not having peeked over the high-rise apartment blocks, all I got was a voicemail informing me that there would be no one in the office for another two hours. No emergency number, of course. I cursed loudly. Then cursed again.

The roar of a motor bike brought me out of my stupor. Without thinking too carefully, I ran for the door of the shop, shouting "Hey, hold on a minute," over and over hoping he would hear me above the sound of the bike. Fortunately, he hadn't put his helmet on at that stage. It was one of those full helmets thingies with the smoky visor. God, could this guy get any sexier? I had a quick vision of him totally naked, apart from the helmet, plowing my ass. I shook my head to dislodge the image.

He switched off the bike. And waited.

"I'm sorry. I need you."

"Everyone says that." I assumed he meant it as a joke. "Let me guess. The agency either doesn't have anyone else available. Or, there's no one in the office yet to take your call."

"Number two," I said dejectedly.

"So, suddenly I'm acceptable. I'm no longer too big or too scary." His sarcasm cut me.

"Looks that way."

He went to put his helmet on. "Thanks, but no thanks."

"Hold on." I made the mistake of grabbing his arm. Feeling his warm skin, I never wanted to let go. He merely stared at my audacity in touching him and I removed my fingers as if I'd been burned.

"No one touches the goods unless I say so."

"I'm sorry. I thought you were going to ride off."

"I was."

"Look, hear me out. Please. Come back into the shop for a moment."

He got off the bike, striding ahead of me as if he owned the place. At that moment, I guess he did, because without someone to deliver the flowers, I was sunk.

Leaning against the counter as if he knew he had all the cards, I shifted uneasily on my feet. "Um, first, I'd like to say how sorry I am at the confusion. And for the things I said earlier. But, I'm desperate. I have all these blooms to box or wrap. It will take all morning. I need someone to deliver them. No way can I do the boxing and deliveries on my own. I stand to lose a lot of money if I can't get them out."

"A shitload of money, I'd say."

I ignored his interruption and hoped he had a romantic streak buried somewhere in that totally hot body of his. Maybe around the area of his massive pecs. "A lot of people will be disappointed if they don't receive their flowers today."

He snorted derisively. "Just a lot of romantic bullshit created by florists to line their pockets."

"You don't celebrate Valentine's Day?"

"Do I look like the sort of guy who'd send roses? Do I look like the sort of guy someone would send flowers to?"

My mouth went into overdrive. "I'd send you flowers." Shit! Did I actually say that out loud? I'd as good as propositioned him. I closed my eyes in readiness for his homophobic outburst.

"Would you expect me to send you roses in return?"

Was I hearing correctly? "No. It has to come naturally. If it's forced, then it's insincere."

"Like all this shit," he said, glancing around the shop. "People expect it and are miserable if they don't get it."

He had me there. "I guess so."

"See ya."

The asthma attack was instant. I couldn't breathe. It always happened when I was stressed to the max. I staggered against the counter, knocking a few small items on the floor in my struggle to get to the drawer that contained my inhaler. I'd kept the attacks mostly in check over the years and had become careless about carrying the inhaler with me at all times. I fumbled at the drawer but the constricted breathing was too much and I sank to my knees.

The intruder was beside me, attempting to help me to my feet, asking what he could do. I pointed to the drawer, gasping "Inhaler." I sat heavily on the floor, my back to the wall while he rummaged amongst the rubbish and delivery dockets.

"You really should keep your shop more tidy," he said impatiently. Finally, he wrenched the drawer out and tipped it upside down, scattering the contents everywhere, but it had the desired effect. I grabbed the inhaler and took a shot. When it worked only partially, I did it again. My breathing slowly returned to normal.

He kept an eye on me as he gathered up the detritus strewn about the floor, stacking it away neatly before returning the drawer to its rightful place. Then he turned his attention to me again. "You okay?"

"Just an asthma attack," I wheezed. "Mainly get them when I'm stressed."

"Should I call the paramedics?"

"I don't have time to deal with them right now. I have work to do." I attempted to stand up as it was highly undignified to be on the floor while conversing with a stranger. In the end, he had to help me to my feet.

"Thanks."

"Well, if you're sure you're all right…"

"Perfectly fine."

"I'll be on my way then."

He turned to go. The panic started again. "Wait."

He stopped, turning to face me. He was my only hope. "I'll give you whatever you want. Just stay and help me."

My groveling must have amused him. "Anything?"

"With the usual provisos. I won't kill anyone for you. As long as it's within my power, anything. And don't think you can sock me for exorbitant wages, there's only a thin profit margin on this stuff. But…I'll up your hourly rate fifty per cent. Is that fair?"

"Plus you'll give me whatever I want at the end of the day?"

"If I can."

He walked over and slapped me on the back. "You got a deal. Call me Ryder, with a Y."

I guess that was better than Blade, with a switch.

"Christopher." I sheepishly retrieved the shears to get back to pruning the roses in preparation for boxing them. Ryder saw me and I flushed with embarrassment.

"You're a gutsy little bastard, I'll grant you that."

"Do you have any other clothes to…um…cover up?"

"Not a one,' he said as if proud of the admission. "Or none I can lay my hands on readily. "I've got a leather jacket under the bike seat."

I sighed. "I guess that will have to do."

"You think I'm that frightening?"

I think you're a walking wet dream, but I didn't say it. "Some people will probably find you intimidating."

"That's not the whole story, is it?"

"No," I admitted. I decided it was best to be honest even if it meant Ryder fled. "Look, this was once an area full of gangs and a bit of violence, so you may frighten some of the older inhabitants."

"I get that," he said.

"But, since the neighborhood has been cleaned up and new people have moved into the area, well, there are a lot of gay men who are the recipients of these Valentines."

"You think fags will what? Go all nelly when they see me? Want to blow me?"

Well, that was straight to the point. "I can't have you beating up my customers."

"You really do have a low opinion of me, don't you? Based entirely on your misconceptions."

"Yeah, I admit it. Just so you don't have the same misconceptions about gay men."

"I have met fags before, you know."

"Okay, I get it. But stop using that word. It's offensive."

"So you're a fag, too?"

"Yeah, I'm gay. My money not good enough for you? Think you'll catch the gay bug from me?"

"Whoa. Take it easy. You're scary when you get riled. Look, I know how to play the game. I can be charming. I can flirt a little. But I know where to draw the line. As long as no one touches, then we'll be okay. You wouldn't expect any less of a female if she was doing your deliveries, would you?"

"No, I wouldn't."

"That's settled then."

It might have been as far as he was concerned, but my opinion was still open.

We spent the next couple of hours getting the deliveries together. I have to give him credit, Ryder was easy to work with and he earned his money. He swept up, helped sort the deliveries into adjacent streets using Google Maps on my laptop, and even proved a satisfactory barista when my early morning clients started appearing on their way to work. The eyebrows of a few of the gay guys shot skywards when they saw Ryder in all his magnificence working the coffee machine. I saw a few of them texting while waiting in line. I had to smile, he was good for business. It was all very well meeting him in the friendly environment of the shop, surrounded by hundreds of blooms and potted plants, but it remained to be seen if the reaction would be the same when people opened their front doors to him unprepared.

I listened carefully, forced to admit he handled the blatant propositions from one or two of the men with skill. No one left feeling belittled or slighted. I noticed a few new faces – mainly gay – pop up that morning. Word had spread. During a lull, he came over to help me again. "Is it always this busy?"

"Valentine's Day is always busy. Most days I don't have as much to do and I can concentrate on the coffees until the workers have left. You, however, seem to have attracted a fan base."

"You mean those fags who kept asking for my phone number?

I glared at him.

"Sorry. Gay guys."

"If it gets you down, tell them you're taken."

"What? You mean tell them I got a girlfriend?"

"Well, do you?" I wanted to ask. Instead, I said, "They'll probably think they can change you if you tell them that."

"So, I should say I got a boyfriend?"

"A little better, but they'll start asking about whether you have an open relationship or whether you cheat on him."

"I don't go in for cheating."

"Um, good to know, but we're talking self-preservation here. This is for your own protection. Just stick with saying you're taken."

"Got it, boss."

I know he was being sarcastic but even play acting at being that little bit subservient got my cock aching. Stupid fantasies of me tapping that hot ass had me creaming pre-cum in my briefs. As if.

As the coffee crowds built up again, more new faces appearing, I had a few regulars take me aside to ask, "Who is he? Where have you been hiding him?"

I freely admitted he was only here for the day, much to the disappointment of a number of customers.

Eventually, the early morning crowds dispersed and the early morning book browsers began appearing. These were more elderly and much more likely to frighten but, after I gave him a crash course in my intricate swap book system, the majority fell under his spell as well. I must admit, watching him at work made the time fly by, until it was time for him to make his first run. I didn't want it to be so early it woke people although they wouldn't remain grumpy for long. Who could when presented with a beautiful bouquet of red roses meaning that someone is thinking of them? But I had a swag to try to deliver before some guys headed off to work. I'd been given the thumbs up by their lovers that it would be a good time to spring the surprise. I just hoped none of them were in the throes of cheating when Ryder turned up.

He headed off in the nifty little refrigerated van that Uncle Ben had purchased eons ago. It probably needed updating but I just didn't have the need for it. I used it more to deliver hot meals to some of the neighbors when they got ill, and to run people to the doctor, or other such tasks.

It was still with some trepidation that I sent him off. Sure enough, less than thirty minutes later the first call came in. "It's about that mountain man you sent with the roses," the voice began.

"I'm so sorry. Please accept my profuse apologies."

"Whatever for? I'm just ringing to say he's an absolute delight, an asset to your company."

"Thank you so much for your feedback," I said, so surprised I actually stuttered.

There were a lot more calls, all of them in the same vein although a few assumed the worst and had offered money incentives to return after the deliveries, still others asking for his phone number. I thanked them for their feedback while deflecting their more personal requests. Later, when I thought about it, I wondered whether Ryder might not be all he seemed and that he may appreciate the monetary offers. I would have to check.

When he returned much sooner than I expected, I was concerned he'd decided to throw it all in. But, no, he'd made the deliveries and was back for more. Once I'd ascertained all was okay, telling him to help himself to one of the sodas in the small fridge behind the counter, or to a coffee, I broached the subject. "Seems you've created quite a stir."

He laughed. "You'd be amazed how many of them think I'm your boyfriend."

That did surprise me. "Really?"

"Really."

"Then you probably won't be all that surprised that men are ringing to ask whether you're available. A small number of women as well."

"Available?"

"To strip at private parties. Or else, for a more intimate one-on-one."

"What did you tell them?"

"That you didn't do that sort of thing."

"So why are you telling me?"

"Just to let you know. It's the way you dress. Too provocative."

"Your customers like it."

"I'll bet they do." I said it under my breath because I thought it made me sound jealous. "But I wanted to let you know in case…um…you know…you want to follow up."

He seemed surprised. "So, what, you now think I'm a whore? You really need to work on your social skills, dude."

"It's just that some of the guys from around here used to turn tricks to save enough money to get themselves out of the ghetto."

"Don't assume, dude."

His attitude turned cold and he barely spoke to me until the next lot of deliveries were packed in the van. I had to make peace so I went outside and tapped on his window. He wound it down – yeah, the van was that old – and I was distressed to see the hurt on his face. "No, I don't think you're a whore, but I know nothing about you and I thought you might need the money."

"I don't mind putting in a hard day's work and be paid a decent wage for it and, yeah, sure I know some dudes are reduced to selling themselves, but it ain't me. I'd starve first."

"I know. I'm sorry."

"Okay. Let's forget it. I don't want to spoil the day. When I get back, we'll pretend it never happened."

He wound up the window before I could reply and I had to step quickly out of the way as he took off.

Back in the shop, the phone was ringing incessantly. Fortunately, most of the roses had been sorted. I always overstock because there are usually last-minute panic requests, mostly from people who'd forgotten the important occasion. I was fielding a few of those already, although some of them came with the request that I send a certain delivery man as if I had dozens of them working for me.

Ryder was as good as his word when he returned, his infectious good mood returned. I eagerly awaited his each return when he shared the funny little adventures he'd experienced and the foibles of the customers. None of the tales were vicious or humiliating to my clients, they were merely human and endearing, and often very funny. I dreaded that the day would end all too soon.

The orders, and requests for Ryder, kept on coming. They weren't all Valentine's Day requests. A group of office girls were farewelling one of their own who was off to have a baby, another group were celebrating a retirement, but the common factor was they wanted eye candy to make the occasion perfect. The testament to just how perfect he made it was the string of congratulatory phone calls. I kept a tab on them, calculating he had done more for the business in just one day than any amount of publicity I'd tried in the past five years. If only I could keep him. For the shop, I mean.

It was after seven when Ryder returned from his final delivery still as perky as ever. I hated him for it because I was exhausted. All I wanted was to climb the stairs and fling myself down on my bed and sleep. The shop was almost denuded of flowers. There would be a good amount to bank in the morning because I was simply too tired to take myself to the night deposit. I'd already counted out Ryder's wages, happy to pay them.

"Help yourself to whatever you want to drink," I said, airily waving my hand in the direction of the machine and the fridge. Here are your wages and I'll be buggered if you don't deserve twice as much. I have added a little bonus on top of the agreed amount. Just a sign of my appreciation for all you've done."

"I didn't do much. I just had fun."

I wasn't about to argue. "I need some sleep."

"Not just yet. You owe me."

"What?"

"You promised to deliver on anything I asked. Within reason."

"I did, didn't I? Okay, what is it you want? Don't make it too difficult as I'm about to drop."

"Take me to dinner."

"What?"

"Take me to dinner."

"I would love to. Just not tonight." Was this a date or was he just hungry? He seemed disappointed. "Will you take a rain check? I won't be much company tonight."

"Yeah, you look buggered. Okay, it's a deal, but I want a deposit so you don't renege on the deal."

"A deposit, like ten per cent of the cost of the meal?"

"Are you always this clueless?" he asked.

I was about to take offence when he swept me in his arms, almost crushing me, and planted a kiss, forcing his tongue between my lips. I was so startled I opened my mouth in surprise and he was in. It took a few moments for it to register that this amazing man was actually pashing me. I could feel his hard cock pressing against my stomach, mine equally hard in reciprocation. I couldn't believe my luck. I had to be hallucinating from lack of sleep.

When we pulled apart, Ryder looked me in the eyes as if searching for some secret. "Wow. I knew you'd be good but not that good. Damn, dude. That kiss was dynamite. I'll be in touch."

He turned and walked away, adjusting his crotch as I could see reflected in the shop window, muttering 'damn' under his breath a number of times. Damn was right. But no matter how excited I was, I needed my sleep. My dick would just have to wait its turn. The time wasn't right the next morning either because I slept in and was almost too late to the markets to pick up new stock. It wasn't until I was back at the shop I had time to reappraise my situation. It seemed lonelier somehow, even though I had worked solo for the past eight years except for the odd occasions, such as Mother's Day, when I needed help with the deliveries. At least I had something to look forward to – the promised dinner.

That fantasy was quashed when I rang the agency to see if I could get a contact number for Ryder. Or, failing that, give him such favorable feedback that if he heard about it he might ring. Molly answered the phone. I had built up a rapport with her over the years and if any of the staff were likely to be forthcoming with personal information about Ryder it was her. As soon as she realized who was calling, Molly went into super apology mode. "Oh, Christopher, I'm so very sorry." She went on in much the same vein for so long I had to interrupt. It didn't stop her. "It's unforgivable but I do hope you managed."

"Yes, quite well, thank you. That chap you sent around was absolutely wonderful at his job."

"What? Who was quite wonderful?"

"Ryder. I never did get his last name. He was so good he increased my business."

"Christopher, what are you talking about? We sent Ken. You said you liked him last year so we thought he was a good fit again this time."

My head was spinning. "Ken? But he never turned up."

"I know. That's what I've been apologizing about. He was involved in a car accident on his way to your shop."

"Oh, my God. Is he all right?"

"Just a mild concussion. How is it you don't know? Did my secretary not ring you?"

"No. Not a word."

"I'll kill her, that's what I'll do."

I got off the phone as fast as I could, wondering who the stranger had been. Had I been taken for a ride? I scanned the shop to see if anything was missing. I laughed at my stupidity; there was nothing here worth stealing. Shit! The day's takings which I'd been too tired to bank. Ryder had offered to deposit them for me. Thank heavens, I refused his offer. Come to think of it, he looked a little put out when I told him I'd do it myself. He watched me lock the takings in the bottom drawer under the counter. I felt for my keys, the bottom falling out of my stomach at the treachery. My hands shook uncontrollably so that it took time to wrench the drawer open. To my surprise, the canvas bag was still there. And still contained the cash. Even more surprising, the unopened envelope containing Ryder's wages was next to it. Now I was puzzled. Who was that Good Samaritan?

As the week progressed, it looked less and less likely Ryder was going to keep our date. I didn't hear from him. I wasn't exactly heartbroken, I hadn't known him long enough, but I was pissed off. I had no right to be. I began to take my lousy mood out on my customers, especially poor Mrs. Melito who was trying again to set me up with her nephew Joey. "He's such a nice quiet boy. The two of you will get along like spaghetti and Bolognese. Why don't you come to dinner so I can introduce you?" After Ryder the last thing I wanted was a 'quiet boy.'

Other patrons complained that my coffee making skills were not up to the standard of 'that gorgeous barista' I had working on Valentine's Day. What they meant was that I was not up to his standard. I knew that, they didn't have to rub it in.

Is it possible to miss someone you don't even know well? I did. Terribly. One kiss, that's all it took. There was a lot of sighing in the boring weeks that followed. My performance in the shop was lackluster. Let's face it, my life was lackluster. About a month after Valentine's Day I was on my knees sweeping up the glass from an inexpensive vase a clumsy customer had knocked over. It had shattered into a million pieces and I was still finding small slivers in the most unlikely places. I didn't want anyone cutting themselves so, in a quiet moment, I was examining every little nook and cranny where the glass could be lurking.

I heard someone enter the store and cursed under my breath. It wasn't a good look for the shop owner to be down on his knees among the shrubs and flowers. I felt a presence behind me. "Did you miss me?" I froze. It couldn't be. I was so unprepared for this moment, I turned and sprang to my feet, grabbing his face and planting the most passionate kiss on his mouth that I could summon. It must have done the trick because his face was flushed when our lips parted.

"Whew," he smiled. "I'll take that as a yes."

Having regained my composure, I attempted to make my voice drip with displeasure. "What are you doing here?"

"Coming to claim my prize."

"And what was the meaning of not taking your wages? You earned them. More than earned them." Ryder went behind the coffee machine and began making us both one of his specials. "Make yourself at home," I said sarcastically.

"I didn't think you'd mind." He smiled, and my anger melted away like autumn snow.

What this man did to me. "I don't. I'm just pissed off, that's all."

"Yeah, I thought you might be. I can explain."

"It better be good."

"I had to leave town in a hurry."

"Cops? Spooks? Drug cartel you owe money?"

"You really do think the best of me, don't you?"

"What was I supposed to think?"

"Set your mind at ease. None of the above."

"So, why didn't you ring? You took my phone number."

"I lost my mobile."

"I'm in the phone book."

"Look," he said with a certain exasperation. "I was in a rather out of the way place with no way of contacting you. I'm sorry. I'm here now, that's all that's important. If that's not good enough, I'll leave now."

"No," I blurted. "Don't go."

"I missed you, too," he said, and wrapped his arms around me.

"Who are you?"

"I told you who I am."

"I thought the agency sent you. Now I know they didn't."

"Yeah, that was a bit naughty of me."

"Naughty? You let me think you were sent by the employment agency. You could have been a thief, a murderer, anything."

"Turns out I wasn't."

"Lucky for me. Lucky for my customers."

"Really lucky for me. I was trying to find an address around here. It was early in the morning and you were the only place with a light on. When I saw you working at the rear of the shop I thought I'd ask directions or see if you had a directory or something. But you took one look and immediately took me for–"

"Okay, I don't need to be reminded."

"Once that was cleared up, you thought I was the delivery guy. I didn't want to disappoint you."

"Disappoint me. I didn't know who the fuck you were. How could you disappoint me?"

"Point is, I thought you were really cute."

"Yeah, pull the other one, it chimes."

He tilted my chin up so I was looking him in the eyes. "Don't put yourself down. You've got gorgeous eyes. And your kiss would lure any man to hell."

I'm so shallow, I preened at the praise. "Is that why you hung around?"

"I hung around because I thought you were cute. Then I found out you were funny, and intelligent, and I had fun with you that day. More fun than I've had in a long, long time."

"I'll take cute. I'll take intelligent. I'll even take fun. But you…look at you, you're fuckin' gorgeous. You could have anyone you want. Anyone at all."

"You know how boring that is?"

I couldn't help the sarcasm, "Aw, poor widdle Ryder. So gorgeous all he has to do is snap his fingers and people fall at his feet. Life must be so difficult." He swatted the back of my head. "Oww!"

"You needed help. I wasn't doing anything that day. I could be myself. By closing time, I got to like you."

"Are you even gay?"

He shrieked in mock horror. "Do I look like a fag? With this body?"

I beat him on the chest with my fist. "That's not an answer. Maybe you're just bi curious."

He pulled me closer and shoved his hand down my trousers, gripping my rock hard cock in his fingers. "I think it's just a phase I'm going through. Maybe you could help test it out."

"Are you seriously suggesting you want to have sex with me?"

I was premature because he said in all seriousness, "No, I'm not." That knocked the wind out of my confidence. "I'm seriously suggesting that I want to get to know you better and make love to you." That knocked even more wind out of me.

"Are you for real, or am I hallucinating from sniffing too many roses?"

"Why don't you take me to dinner tonight and find out?"

"Are you asking me on a date?"

"Believe it or not."

Ryder stayed with me, serving coffees and exchanging paperbacks just like he did before. Many of the customers seemed genuinely pleased to see him again, especially the few gay men who popped in on a weekday. We chatted amiably and, yes, mysterious as he was, there was an affinity between us. When the conversation dried up, I didn't feel uncomfortable, and sometimes I'd look up, a huge grin on my face, to catch him staring at me, smiling.

"Where would you like to go for dinner?" I asked.

"Nothing fancy. I'm not a food snob."

"Thai suit you?"

"Love Thai food."

I rang and booked a table for two at Thai Phoon. Terrible name for a restaurant although no one ever forgot it, but their food was amazing, especially their Massaman Beef Curry. Ryder left mid-afternoon as he had 'things to do,' he said. It didn't matter because I would see him again in a few hours. Stupidly, I didn't grab his phone number before he left, so it was with a little trepidation that I waited for him to pick me up. With five minutes to spare I heard his motorbike pull into the small parking space in front of the shop. I locked up and went out to join him. Damn, if he didn't look just as hot in a shirt as he did naked to the waist. He scrubbed up very well indeed.

I'd intended taking the van but after removing his helmet and greeting me with an open-mouthed kiss which threw me as I still couldn't believe this man would be interested in a little squirt like me, he handed me a helmet to join him on the back of the bike. Sad to say I'd never been on a bike before. My heart raced at the thought, especially as I'd be up close and personal to his leather clad ass.

"Looking good, dude," he said as he appraised my tight leather trousers. We would have looked like book ends if I'd been bigger, now it just looked as if we were mates – or fuck buddy bikers. I could live with that.

I'd held my breath when he watched me walk out of the shop because any sign of humor or twitch of embarrassment and I would have gone back inside and changed. Instead, as I straddled his bike behind him, he ran his hand up my leather-clad thigh. "I like it," he murmured. I didn't need to give him directions as he looked up the address for the Thai Phoon before he arrived. Besides, there was no way to make myself heard through the helmet and all the traffic noise.

Tentatively, I placed my arms around him, wondering if that was the correct protocol. I didn't wonder long because he pulled me into a tighter grip so that my crotch was wedged against his ass. I was instantly hard and he felt it because he kept pushing back against me. The short ride to the restaurant was an exhilarating mixture of speed and the horniness of having a hot man just a leather thickness away. What's more, the hot man seemed to be in the mood to play.

At the restaurant we were seated at a table private enough that we didn't have to pull any punches as we chatted about our lives. Ryder's was the exact opposite of mine. Where I was dull and timid, he was extrovert and exciting. He was such an expert storyteller I was right there with him as he told of his experiences. I was so enthralled I found myself leaning forward to get more involved in his narrow escapes, his hair-brained schemes, and his travels. I had never traveled farther than from my parents' farm to the city. I never took holidays although I had a drawer full of tempting brochures tucked away in my front counter. If business was slow I would sometimes take them out and daydream.

"Why haven't you ever traveled?" Ryder asked. He planted his boot in my crotch. Fortunately, the tablecloth hid our flirtation. I'd rubbed my booted foot against his leg earlier while he was speaking and now he retaliated, upping the ante tenfold. I groaned as my cock stiffened for…I'd lost count how many times, it seemed to be in a constant state of arousal. I think if I'd suggested we leave at that very moment, he would have agreed, but we'd ordered and as if to protest the thought, my stomach grumbled.

"Too busy with the shop," I replied.

"You mean you've never taken a break?"

"It's not like I don't want to visit all those places overseas, but it doesn't sound like much fun doing it on your own."

Ryder's face lit up. "Why not come with me?"

I was going to mutter all the excuses I always brought up when people asked. Adrian had invited me along to accompany him and his boyfriend to Italy one year, but I didn't want to intrude on what was a second honeymoon for them. Then it hit me; the subtext of what Ryder was saying.

"You intend hanging around then?"

"I can't see any reason to move on. Not when I've finally found what I've been searching for."

"What's that?"

He slapped me lightly on the side of the head.

"You better stop doing that if you want this friendship to last," I warned.

"I'll stop if you promise to stop being obtuse."

"I'm not," I complained. "I have no idea what you've been searching for."

"You, you dickhead. I've been searching for you."

"You didn't know I existed until about a month ago. How could you have been searching for me?"

"I was searching for Mr. Right. I knew I'd find him one day and I'd recognize him instantly."

"You believe in love at first sight?"

"The moment I saw you, I knew you were the one. Or one of the ones. I just prayed you didn't have a boyfriend because that would have broken my heart. And I knew you liked me because even when you stood up to me with those ridiculous pruning shears, you were hard in your pants."

"You noticed, did you?"

"It was hard to miss." He smirked at the power he had over me.

Our main course arrived and the conversation was put on hold. I'd ordered for both of us because Ryder was unfamiliar with the cuisine, except in takeaway joints where he could just point at the dishes pictured on the wall.

"Oh, man," he moaned after the first few mouthfuls, "This is glorious. What did you say it's called?"

"Massaman curry. It's Muslim in origin."

"I can see I have a new favorite place to eat. Is all their food this good?"

"Just about."

It made me feel good to watch him eat with such pleasure.

Once the dishes were cleared, Ryder reached across the table and held my hand. I looked about nervously in case anyone was watching. "Hey, look at me, Christopher." It was the first time he'd used my name and it snapped my attention back to him. I was pleased he hadn't called me Chris. "I think we could be on the threshold of something really good here. But you've gotta trust me. Okay?"

"I do."

"Can I stay the night?"

"Did you bring a toothbrush?"

"Damn, I forgot."

"No worries. I've got a spare."

I quickly paid for the meal, Ryder left a hefty tip, and we were back at the shop faster than I would have imagined possible. I allowed Ryder to park his motorbike in the small garage to the side of the shop before unlocking the door. I ushered him inside, and then we made our way upstairs to my comfortable apartment. "Oh, I like this set-up," Ryder said, testing the lounge and the dining table chairs. "Is the bed as comfortable?"

"Try it for yourself," I said pointing him in the right direction.

He was as frisky as a puppy, flopping about the bed, holding out his arms until I joined him. I lay on top of his hard muscular body without any fear of crushing him. He pulled me down for a kiss, and then another, continuing until my lips were swollen and my cock was painfully hard in my trousers.

"I think we might be more comfortable without all these constricting clothes," he said.

I couldn't agree fast enough but leather is not the easiest clothing to remove in a hurry, not helped by the fact we constantly nudged each other accidentally, falling on the bed laughing more often than removing any constricting article. Eventually, however, we were both naked. If I'd felt inadequate before, seeing Ryder totally naked made me self-conscious. I tried to hide my body behind my hands until I could disappear under the sheet. He was having none of that.

"Let me see." He sat astride my hips to look down at me. "Beautiful," he mumbled. I wasn't about to spoil the evening by disagreeing. He ran his hands over my chest and stomach. I had a one-pack to his six. A slightly above-average cock to his monster. My sphincter clutched in terror at the thought of him burying that inside me. There was no argument, I was puny, he was buff. "You are exactly the sort of man I'm attracted to, Christopher." He stopped me when I went to object. "I don't want to sleep with someone with a body like mine. That's just a form of narcissism."

He leaned down to lick my nipples before nipping them gently with his teeth. My nipples are one of my sensitive points and I thrashed about attempting to dislodge him, but he wasn't going anywhere. When he decided he'd spent enough time on my chest he ran his tongue down my stomach to my navel. My cock was shouting 'yoo hoo, down here,' concerned it wasn't going to get any attention. It needn't have worried because Ryder licked my balls, nudging them aside with his nose, before turning his focus to my dick which was dribbling with delight.

He lapped at the piss hole, cleaning all the pre-cum away. "You taste so good," he whispered.

I wanted to return the favor but he held me down. "Let me this time," he said. That implied there would be other times so I wouldn't have to cram a lifetime into one evening. I relaxed to concentrate on the feelings he was creating in my groin. I don't know about you, but I never think of guys built like the proverbial brick shithouse as being anything other than the sort of man who has his dick sucked. I never see them as dick suckers, but here was Ryder, his cheeks hollowed, putting everything he had into blowing me. I watched his handsome head bobbing up and down on my prick, amazed it wasn't me being choked on his monster. I guessed that would happen soon enough.

Ryder was an expert cocksucker. I'd never had better. He did such wonderful things to my body I was afraid if he kept it up he'd need to scrape me off the ceiling. I moaned, I wriggled, I tore at the bed as he took my prick right down his throat until his nose rested in my pubes. No way was I going to be able to reciprocate to that extent.

"Stop. Now." I commanded. It was more abrupt than I intended but if he'd kept up his blow job I would have lost my load in the next thirty seconds.

He ceased and I felt his cock twitch against my leg. Hmm, maybe it was worth a go. "On your back, legs in the air, hold them still."

"Yes, Sir." He couldn't take up the position fast enough, spreading his ass cheeks so I could marvel at his beautiful tight entrance. I rubbed my nose in the crack before my tongue began lapping against the hole. Ryder gripped the back of my head, holding me into his ass crack until I was afraid of smothering. As best I could, I sucked his ring then pushed my tongue as far into the groove as possible. I slapped his big beefy buttocks drawing even more groans from him. If we repeated this evening, I had a few surprises to spring involving handcuffs, butt plugs, and a paddle. Nothing hardcore BDSM, but enough to make sex play a little more interesting.

After I'd spit lubed his ass with my tongue, I surfaced for air. I couldn't believe this man, this wet dream on legs, lay flat on his back, his ass raised ready for my cock. I leaned over to the bedside table to retrieve condoms and lube from the drawer. Ryder did not take his eyes off my face, his eyes hooded and filled with lust, the like of which I'd never seen before. I could get to love that.

I sheathed my prick and greased the condom. I was about to prep Ryder's ass when he croaked in a voice fogged with desire, "Just ram it in. I want it to hurt." I wasn't one to argue. Placing the head at the puckered entrance, I swirled my prick around to spread the lube to give me better access. I began to squeeze into his ass muscles. God, he was tight. Finally, the head of my prick broke through and Ryder gasped briefly. I stopped to allow him time to adjust. When the creases of pain in his face subsided, I began to push in slowly until he grabbed my ass and pulled me all the way inside him.

I almost screamed as the steamy paradise wrapped around my cock. This had been a dream of mine for so long: a muscle god impaled on my prick, and here it was in all its glory. The feeling was so intense I knew I wouldn't last long. I picked up the pace, watching Ryder's face intently, attempting to read his moods. I wrapped my hand around his cock and began to pump in time to my thrusts. He pushed back as if he wanted even more of me inside him.

"Oh, God, Christopher. You feel so good."

"Not half as good as my cock feels wedged in your ass."

"Fuck me hard. Please."

He asked so nicely, how could I refuse? I rammed so energetically his body moved up the bed until he banged against the head board. I couldn't get enough of his choice ass. All too soon I felt his balls clutch and he screamed obscenities as his spunk blew across his stomach, as high as his chest and neck. The extra traction from the grip in his sphincter muscles, forced me over the edge and I shot my load into the latex enclosing my cock. I shoved the last few spurts into him as hard as I could considering that my entire body felt as if it were melting. I collapsed on top of him, unconcerned that I was rubbing against the puddled spunk on his belly.

He kissed my eyelids. "Who would have guessed?"

I smiled sleepily. "I sure wouldn't to look at you."

"That's my secret," he said. "But I do like to top from time to time."

"Not sure I can take that weapon between your legs without a lot of practice."

"I promise I'll be gentle. But not tonight."

"Meaning you won't be gentle tonight? Or you'll fuck me some other time?"

"Yeah," he said, not answering the question. He was dozing before I could even query him further. I pulled out, disposing of the condom in the trash can beside the bed, and lowered his legs gently onto the mattress. Ryder turned on his side and, not being one for assigned stereotypical role play, I snuggled my back against him until he wrapped his arms around me and I fell asleep like a bear cub in hibernation.

We woke twice during the night. The first occasion, I managed to get most of his cock into my mouth but not without a lot of gagging and mucous snorting out my nose before he shot a load down the back of my throat. I was gonna need a lot more practice if I was to tame that fuckpole.

The second time, Ryder snuggled against me and my cock, sensing another opportunity, went for gold. The lovemaking this time was more leisurely and lasted a great deal longer to the satisfaction of both of us. When I pulled out to dispose of the condom, Ryder grabbed my cock and squeezed. "I think I could become addicted to you." I wasn't sure whether he meant just my prick or the whole me.

By morning, I'd admitted as much to him as well. Naturally, a shower together to wipe last night's crust from our bodies, led to more amorous play and I made another attempt to take his cock all the way down my throat, again just shy of success, but with less gagging. He took the opportunity to insert his finger in my ass as he soaped me up.

Over a leisurely breakfast – it was Saturday so I didn't have to go to the flower markets – it was difficult to know what to say.

"Are you embarrassed?" Ryder asked.

"Hell, no."

"What's the matter then?"

"I'm just trying to figure out a way to ask you to stay."

"You offering me a job?"

"If you like. I loved having you in the shop. If your presence means extra customers, then I can afford you."

"I don't have to wear a uniform, do I?"

"Just those sexy leather jeans."

"Nothing else?"

"Your boots. Too many used syringes lying around the streets."

"Might be cold in winter."

"I'll get you a leather vest, don't want to cover that six-pack of yours. You could play percussion on it."

He laughed. "Probably too early to be talking about love."

"Probably."

"What about me moving in?"

"Would we have to indulge in wild, animal sex every night?"

"Absolutely."

"When can you move your stuff in?"

We carried on like two lovesick teenagers. I'm not a fool, I knew there would be hurdles to overcome. For starters, I knew as little about him as he knew about me, but I didn't mind finding out while on the job. I'd make the most of it while it worked and, if it didn't, I'd consider myself blessed to have spent time with Ryder. I had a good feeling about it though.

I went downstairs to open the shop leaving Ryder upstairs in his sexy briefs. I sold a few coffees, re-arranged the displays, and generally caught up on paperwork, content to know Ryder was upstairs.

It was about ten, during a lull in sales, when the bell attracted my attention away from paying bills via my laptop. It was Mrs. Melito. At last, I could tell her I had a boyfriend and deflect her matchmaking.

"Morning, Mrs. Melito. How are you today?"

She'd brought back some paperbacks she wanted to swap. She was a Georgette Heyer addict and had read the complete oeuvre at least three or four times.

"Not so good today, Christopher. I worry about Joey. He goes away without a word. What sort of boy does that? Not a good boy. Perhaps it's just as well you never met him. You need a man you can…" The words died in her throat. She had a look of shock on her face. I turned to see what had taken her breath away. Ryder was standing all but naked, except for his cute red briefs, at the bottom of the stairs. "Auntie Francesca, what are you…?"

"Joey?"

"You're Joey Melito? The man I've been avoiding all this time?"

"My prayers have been answered." Mrs. Melito clapped her hands in prayer.

"I thought your name was Ryder."

"Joey is a kid's name. Does this body look like it goes with a name like Joey?"

We were all talking at once until Ryder/Joey put his fingers to his lips and whistled. That got our attention. And an earache. "I'm going upstairs to get dressed. Then we can all sit down and discuss this."

I went over to the coffee counter to play barista, adding a few day-old pastries to a plate, and carried them to the counter. When Ryder came back downstairs, he kissed his aunt on the cheek, then came and stood beside me.

"Is this what it looks like?" Mrs. Melito asked.

"What's it look like?" I asked.

"You should see yourselves," she laughed. "Just like me and Joey's uncle. Couldn't get the smiles off our faces. Not in the forty years we were together. Bless his soul." She crossed herself. "So, is it?"

Joey took my hand and held it. He searched my eyes for a few moments before he said, "Yes, you can stop matchmaking now, Auntie Francesca, I'm officially taken."

Lydian Press

ABOUT THE AUTHOR

Barry Lowe writes about love and sex so he won't forget how to do it. When he's not out doing field research, he's writing about love's wonderful variations for a series of smut eBooks, novels and anthologies for Lydian Press

Go to www.barrylowe.info

OTHER WORKS BY BARRY LOWE

Available in eBook and Print

PLAYS

THE DEATH OF PETER PAN: Gay Historical Romance

NOVELS & ANTHOLOGIES

BUSTING BILLY'S BUTT: A Gay Erotic Romance

Steve and Billy's monogamous relationship has gone stale until Billy, ever the exhibitionist, shows them a way to spice up their sex life.

THE MAJOR AND THE MINERS: A Gay Historical Romance

1930s Australia: Two men from opposite ends of the social spectrum. Is love enough to overcome the obstacles between them?

THE GRAVY TRAIN: A Murder Mystery with Recipes

Someone on the train has an appetite for murder!

A TOUCH OF THE SON: A Gay Novel

Their secret passion will lead them to hell. Will they be able to find their way back?

ROMANCING THE BONE: Gay Romance Erotica

OMG! NOT ANOTHER GAY EROTICA ANTHOLOGY?

ROUGH & READY: Gay Tough Guy Erotica

YOUR BOYFRIEND IS HOT: Gay Cuckold Erotica

BEAR SKIN: Hot Gay Bear Erotica

THE MORE THE MERRIER: Gay Gangbang Erotica

THE BOY IS A BOTTOM: Gay Anal Erotica

COCK-EYED OPTIMISTS: Gay Romance Erotica

BABY, I'M NOT A MONSTER: Gay Vampire and Other Paranormal Erotica

CHRISTMAS CRACKER: Gay Erotica for the Holidays

BUTT BOYS: Gay Anal Erotica

HOW MUCH IS THAT DOGGIE IN THE WINDOW?

BACHELOR BOY

BAD-ASS BOYS

THE BI-WORD

SELECTED SHORT FICTION

Available as eBooks

LOVE WITH A SIDE ORDER OF PELICANS

CHRISTMAS IN JULY

BREEDING MY BOYFRIEND

NEW JOCK IN TOWN

BACHELOR BOY

SUMMER AT RAINBOW COVE

I WAS A MALE NYMPHO FOR THE FBI

HOW MUCH IS THAT DOGGIE IN THE WINDOW?

THE DAY OF THE CLIFFORDS

HE WON'T SEND ROSES

A RED ROSE BEFORE CRYING

PRIDE AND JOY

ROAD HUMP

THE GOOD, THE BAD, AND THE CUDDLY

THE GROOM CLOSET

TUNNEL VISION

HARD ON HIS HEELS

SPIN THE BOTTOM

THE NEW DAD'S CLUB

FOUR ON THE FLOOR

TAGGED BY THE TEAM

WANNA SHARE YOUR HUSBAND

For all Barry's titles please visit his page at: lydianpress.com

Lydian Press is dedicated to bringing you the
finest GLBTQ erotic literature on the web.

Visit us on the web at:
http://lydianpress.com